FROM THE
NANCY DREW FILES

THE CASE: Nancy pursues a cold-hearted criminal across a glacial landscape.

CONTACT: A chance encounter with Alex and Kara Wheeler leads Nancy to a mountain of crime.

SUSPECTS: Anne Bolle—Kara beat her in a prestigious rock-climbing competition . . . and revenge may be her only consolation.

Hank Moody—Owner of the failing Outrageous Adventures, he would love to see his business rivals take a hard fall.

Lisa Ostermann—A stranger who has just joined the expedition, Lisa talks big and she lies big . . . and whatever she's hiding could prove fatal.

COMPLICATIONS: Someone may be out to murder Kara Wheeler, and if Ned doesn't stop paying so much attention to the other woman, Nancy may have to count herself among the suspects.

Books in The Nancy Drew Files® Series

Available from ARCHWAY Paperbacks

Published by POCKET BOOKS

New York London Toronto Sydney Tokyo Singapore

The NANCY DREW

Files™
103

HEART OF ICE

CAROLYN KEENE

AN ARCHWAY PAPERBACK
Published by POCKET BOOKS
New York   London   Toronto   Sydney   Tokyo   Singapore

AN ARCHWAY PAPERBACK *Original*

An Archway Paperback published by
POCKET BOOKS, a division of Simon & Schuster Inc.
1230 Avenue of the Americas, New York, NY 10020

Copyright © 1995 by Simon & Schuster Inc.
Produced by Mega-Books, Inc.

ISBN: 0-671-88194-9

First Archway Paperback printing January 1995

10 9 8 7 6 5 4 3 2 1

NANCY DREW, AN ARCHWAY PAPERBACK and colophon are registered trademarks of Simon & Schuster Inc.

THE NANCY DREW FILES is a trademark of Simon & Schuster Inc.

Cover art by Cliff Miller

Printed in the U.S.A.

IL 6+

HEART OF ICE

Chapter

One

THIS IS GOING to be the best vacation," Nancy Drew said, brushing her reddish blond hair back. "A whole week of skiing in Washington State." Nancy was weaving through the passengers at Chicago's O'Hare airport with Ned Nickerson, her longtime boyfriend.

Ned answered by squeezing Nancy's hand as he dodged a man carrying an overstuffed garment bag. Since Ned went away to college, Nancy and he didn't see each other often. Ned was on winter break now, and they had planned a whole week of skiing, just the two of them.

When they reached the gate, their flight to Tacoma, Washington, was boarding. "Perfect timing," Nancy murmured. A few moments later they walked through the jetway and onto the plane, but when they reached their seats, they found them occupied.

"Excuse me," Nancy said politely. "I think this is my seat."

"Is it?" The man who smiled up at Nancy was young and athletic looking, with bright blue eyes and a nice smile. He checked his boarding pass as the woman and little girl sitting next to him looked up from the Mickey Mouse coloring book. The little girl was adorable, with cinnamon curls and big blue eyes. The woman was a knockout, with long dark hair and deep green eyes.

"You're right," the man said. "We're supposed to be in Eight D, E, and F." He pointed to the three empty seats on the other side of the aisle.

The woman quickly put the crayons back into the box and gathered up her belongings. Within a few minutes, the young family had moved across the aisle.

"Thanks," Ned said.

Nancy plopped down into the aisle seat next to Ned and stowed her carry-on bag under the seat in front of her. After buckling her seat belt, she opened her copy of *Great Outdoors* and began reading an article on skiing.

Ned leaned over and squeezed Nancy's hand in excitement. "This is going to be a great week," he whispered, discreetly nuzzling her neck.

Before long the plane had taken off and reached an altitude of 35,000 feet and was soaring over the plains of South Dakota.

After an hour or so Nancy looked over and noticed that the little girl was snuggled up against her mom, sound asleep, a purple crayon still clenched in her small fist.

"She's adorable," Nancy said, leaning across the aisle. "What's her name?"

"Allison." The woman smiled tenderly at her daughter. "We think she's a keeper."

Nancy laughed. "Do you live in Chicago?" she asked.

"No," the husband answered. "We've been visiting my wife Kara's family for the holidays," he answered as he swirled the ice in his soft drink.

"We live in a little town about thirty miles east of Tacoma called Enumclaw," Kara added.

"I think we drive through Enumclaw on our way to Crystal Falls," Nancy said thoughtfully, sipping her tea.

3

"Oh, you're going skiing?" Kara asked, her eyes bright. "Crystal Falls is a terrific resort. We went skiing there over Thanksgiving and they already had great snow."

Nancy smiled and daydreamed about the skiing. It felt great to leave her detective work behind for six glorious days. At eighteen, Nancy had already established herself as a formidable detective. The daughter of a well-known criminal attorney, Carson Drew, Nancy inherited many cases through her father. She loved solving mysteries, but she had vowed to steer clear of crime on this vacation.

"Do you ski a lot?" Nancy asked, coming out of her dream.

The man laughed. "You could say that. We run a small alpine guide service. Our specialty is alpining—you know, climbing mountains. But we also do rock climbing and skiing."

"Wow," Nancy said. "That sounds like fun. How long have you been in business?"

"Just over a year. But Kara has been climbing seriously for more than ten years." He reached over and took his wife's hand. "She was the top climber in the U.S. before she gave it all up to become a mom."

4

"Oh, Alex," Kara said, embarrassed. "You always make my climbing sound like such a big deal."

"It sounds pretty impressive to me," Ned commented, and Nancy agreed.

"I just love to climb and happen to be good at it," Kara said modestly.

"So how's business?" Nancy asked, changing the subject.

"Great," Alex answered, leaning back and stretching his legs out in front of him. "Clients have been coming to us through word of mouth. Sometimes we have to hire freelance guides because more people sign up for a trip than we expected. A staff writer from *Great Outdoors* magazine is coming on a winter ascent of Mount Rainier with us this week," he said, pointing to the magazine Nancy was holding. "With a little luck, he'll write some positive things about us and we'll really be on our way."

"It'll take more than luck, Alex," Kara said affectionately.

"What do you mean?" Nancy asked, her curiosity getting the best of her.

"Well, on a big, volcanic, glacial mountain like Rainier, you have a lot to worry about—snow bridges, crevasses, avalanches, not to mention your equipment," Kara rattled off. "You really have to know what you're doing."

"But getting to the top amidst all that incredible wilderness beauty must be worth it. It must be a real thrill at the top," Nancy said.

"Oh, there's nothing like it," Kara agreed. "It's the most exhilarating feeling I know."

A little while later the pilot's voice announced their approach to the Tacoma airport.

"Wow, that was fast," Nancy commented as a flight attendant passed by to collect their cups and napkins.

At the baggage claim, Nancy and Ned waited for their luggage with their new friends the Wheelers. As they were gathering their things together Alex handed Nancy a business card. "If you want to stop in on your way back from Crystal Falls, let us know," he said. "Enumclaw is about halfway between the ski resort and Tacoma."

"We've just finished building a little house in the woods. We'd love to have you visit," Kara added warmly, picking up Allison.

"Thanks," Nancy answered, smiling. "We just might do that."

"Goodbye, Allison," Ned called as the Wheelers left the terminal.

Allison grinned and waved. "'Bye," she called back.

"What great people," Nancy commented to Ned. "I feel like we've known them for years."

While Nancy waited for the luggage, Ned went to rent a car. When he came back with the contract and the keys, he noticed their ski equipment still hadn't arrived. The carousel was nearly empty.

"Oh, no," Ned groaned. "Don't tell me our skis are missing."

Nancy sighed. This wasn't the great start to their vacation she had wanted. "That's what it looks like," she answered, frowning.

Twenty minutes later Nancy and Ned learned that their skis had mistakenly been put on a plane to Arizona. The service representative told them that they probably couldn't get the skis to them for a couple of days.

"What should we do?" Ned asked. "We can't exactly hit the slopes without skis."

"We could rent them," Nancy suggested.

Ned put an affectionate arm around Nancy and gave her a squeeze. "That's why I love you,

7

Nan," he said. "You always think positively, and you always have a plan."

After hoisting their bags, Nancy and Ned made their way to the courtesy van that would take them to their rental car. An hour and a half later they had arrived at Crystal Falls Resort.

After checking into their rooms and freshening up, they met again in the lobby of their hotel and headed across the compound to the ski rental shop. When Nancy walked through the door, she noticed right away that there was hardly any gear for sale. As it turned out, virtually any equipment they could ski on was already rented because it was one of the busiest weeks of the year.

Nancy sighed heavily. She and Ned had flown halfway across the country to a great ski resort and now they had no equipment!

"What are we going to do?" Ned asked as they left the shop to go outside.

"I have no idea," Nancy answered. "Our perfect vacation is turning into a disaster."

"No, it isn't," Ned said, stopping to slip both his arms around Nancy's waist. "My vacation is still wonderful, because you're here with me."

"Oh, Ned, of course you're right," Nancy said, resting her hand lightly on the nape of his neck. She stared off at majestic Mt. Rainier with its snow-covered peaks, the only significant mountain for miles. "But what are we going to do for the next— Hey," she cried, suddenly excited. "Let's call Alex and Kara and see if we can go on that Rainier trip!"

"Are you sure, Nan?" Ned asked. "I mean, it's *January*. And Rainier is a big mountain and could be very dangerous to climb."

"Oh, come on, Nickerson. We've both done serious climbing, and we're in good shape."

Ned studied Nancy's face against a backdrop of snow and pines. "All right," he agreed. "If it's what you really want to do, I'm game."

In her room Nancy dialed the number for Alpine Adventures. When Kara answered the phone, Nancy immediately heard the anxiety in her voice. "Kara, it's Nancy Drew."

"Oh, Nancy," Kara said with a sigh.

"Is everything all right?" Nancy asked.

"No," Kara replied. "Somebody has broken into Alpine Adventures—the place has been ransacked!"

Chapter

Two

"WHEN DID IT HAPPEN?" Nancy asked.

"Last night, we think," Kara answered. "Someone smashed a window and stole one of our computers and some of our most expensive gear. The thief also dumped our files—the office is a complete mess."

"Have you called the police?" Nancy asked, wrapping the phone cord around her finger.

"Yes," Kara answered. "Alex called them, and they're on their way." She paused. "Why are you calling? Are you okay?"

"We're fine," Nancy answered, feeling awkward. It certainly wasn't a good time to ask if she and Ned could go on the Rainier trip.

"Are you in town?" Kara prodded.

"No. We're at Crystal Falls. The airline lost our skis, and the rental shop has rented everything worth skiing on. So we were wondering if there might be room for us on the Rainier trip."

"Absolutely," Kara answered, without hesitating. "We'd be thrilled to have you. Why don't you drive over this afternoon. There's no point in paying for your rooms at the resort if you can't ski."

"Are you sure it's not an imposition?" Nancy asked. Even as she spoke, questions about the break-in whizzed through her mind. "We could come tomorrow morning if that'd be better."

"Don't be silly," Kara answered. "It will be nice to have a little moral support. And please plan on having supper with us tonight."

"Wonderful," Nancy agreed. "Should we meet you at the office?"

"Yes, I think that would be best. Just take Route Four-ten to Highway One sixty-four and turn right onto Harding. We're two blocks down on the right. You'll see the sign."

"Great," Nancy responded. "We'll see you in an hour or so."

Fifteen minutes later Nancy and Ned had packed their things and checked out of their hotel. Nancy had even persuaded the inn to refund their money. She'd had to argue with the manager for ten minutes, saying that if the rental shop couldn't provide skis, guests should have the option to check out with a full refund. The manager had finally agreed.

"I feel like we've been traveling for days," Ned grumbled as he settled into the passenger seat of their car.

"Me, too," Nancy answered, and pulled the car onto the highway. "And now we've got the break-in at Alpine Adventures to worry about, too."

Ned sighed. "We're two thousand miles from home and you've managed to find us a crime, Nan," he said.

"I'm sure it won't be anything big," Nancy assured him, "and I'm not going to let anything spoil our fun together."

"Good." Ned smiled, relieved. "Because this is one vacation where I want you all to myself."

After a fifty-minute drive, Nancy and Ned parked in front of 120 Harding in Enumclaw.

The Alpine Adventures office was in a one-story brick building with a handsome wooden sign above the door.

Nancy and Ned walked through the door into a large waiting room. Rustic wooden benches lined one wall, and a few pieces of outdoor equipment hung on pegs behind the counter.

An attractive young woman was sitting on the floor of the room with Allison Wheeler. The little girl was paging through a picture book as the woman sifted through the mess of papers strewn everywhere.

"Hi," she said to Nancy and Ned. She stood up and brushed off her jeans. She was about five feet four and solidly built, with shoulder-length black hair and almond-shaped eyes.

Taking Allison's hand, she walked over to where Nancy and Ned were standing. "I'm Tsu Chung, the assistant guide," she said, introducing herself. "You must be Nancy and Ned."

"We are," Ned replied.

"I'm just trying to make some sense of this mess," Tsu explained. "Though I'm not sure I'm making any progress," she added with a laugh.

"I'm sure you've done a lot," Nancy said to encourage her. Desk drawers were open, with

13

papers strewn everywhere. A power cable for the missing computer lay on one of the desks.

"Kara and Alex are in the gear room with Logan," Tsu continued, pointing to a doorway. "They're with the police."

Just then Kara came through the doorway. "Oh, you're here." She smiled. "Sorry about the mess."

"Don't be silly," Nancy responded, glancing through the door Kara had just come through. Alex and another good-looking man, who Nancy guessed was Logan, were with two police officers. Logan was tall—well over six feet—with broad shoulders, dark curly hair, and dark eyes. "I just hope we're not intruding," Nancy added.

"Not at all," Kara answered. "You were invited and it's comforting to have you here," she added sincerely.

"When did the police get here?" Nancy asked.

"About ten minutes ago," Kara answered, a sudden edge to her voice. "It took them an hour to show up."

Nancy put a comforting hand on Kara's arm. "The important thing is that they're here," she said.

"I'm sure they'll get to the bottom of this," Ned added, gazing at Kara.

"Ned's right," Nancy agreed, not sure she liked the way Ned always stared at Kara.

Just then Logan came out of the storage room. "You must be Nancy Drew and Ned Nickerson," he said heartily. "I'm Logan Miller, Alex's right-hand man."

Nancy and Ned shook hands with Logan. "Looks like you've got quite a mess to straighten out," Nancy said, nodding toward the area where Tsu had been working.

"No kidding." Logan sighed and shook his head. "I don't know why anyone would mess with our paperwork—it's just information about our trips. And as far as we can tell they didn't take any of it."

"When did you realize there had been a break-in?"

"This morning when I came in at eleven-thirty," Logan answered. "We open at noon on Tuesdays and Thursdays," he explained.

"When did you close up last night?" Nancy asked.

"I didn't," he answered. "I was in Olympia for the evening, giving a slide presentation for the Guides' Association," he explained.

"I closed up," Tsu added. "I worked late, until about nine o'clock."

As Tsu finished her sentence, Alex and the police came out of the gear room. "Oh, hi," he said. "Glad you made it. These are Officers Kelley and Fernandez."

The men nodded at Nancy and Ned.

"We'd like to ask you a few questions, Ms. Chung," Officer Fernandez said to Tsu. He was the older of the two officers and seemed to be in charge of the investigation. "Would you care to step into another room?"

"I'd rather stay here, if that's okay," Tsu replied. "I don't have anything to say that these people can't hear."

"What time did you close the office last night?" Officer Kelley asked, pulling a small notebook out of his pocket. He dropped his pencil on the floor, and Logan bent to pick it up for him. "Thanks," Kelley said, a little embarrassed. He was young, maybe twenty-five, and Nancy guessed he was fairly new on the force.

"I was just telling Nancy that I worked until about nine o'clock, doing a gear check."

"A gear check?" Officer Kelley repeated quizzically.

"Yes. We have a trip this weekend and I was making sure everything was in order," Tsu explained.

"I see," Officer Kelley said, nodding. "So you left later than usual, I take it?"

"Yes. I usually leave at around seven o'clock," Tsu responded, folding her arms across her chest.

"And when you left, you locked up?"

Tsu nodded. "I always double-check the door, because the lock is a little funny."

Nancy watched as Officer Kelley wrote "funny lock" down in his notebook.

"Did you notice anything unusual before or as you left?" he asked, looking up.

"No." Tsu shook her head thoughtfully. "Everything was normal."

Officer Kelley scribbled this down, too. Then he flipped his notebook closed and turned toward Alex.

"Looks like a juvenile prank to me," he said, clucking his tongue. "Your gear is probably sitting in somebody's basement right now."

Nancy considered what Kelley had said. Kids would have probably thrown a rock through the large front window to get in. No, she decided, there was more to this than a prank.

"If we get any leads, we'll be sure to let you know," Officer Fernandez said. "And if you hear anything, just call the station and tell Mrs. Loomis you need to speak with us."

"All right." Alex shook the officers' hands before they left.

As soon as the door had closed, Kara spoke. "I don't believe their theory for a second," she said, and Nancy nodded in agreement. She was intrigued by this crime.

"If you don't need us here anymore, Tsu and I have some errands to run," Logan said to Alex.

"Fine," Alex said.

"Would you like to come over for dinner?" Kara asked. "We're having pasta. Ned and Nancy will be there, too."

"I'd never pass up the chance to eat one of your home-cooked meals, Kara," Logan replied with an easygoing grin.

"Me, neither," Tsu agreed. "I'll bring dessert."

"Great." Kara nodded.

"So tell me," Nancy began when she and Ned were alone with the Wheelers. "Why don't you think it was kids who broke into your office?"

"It could be," Kara admitted. "It's just that we've been having an awful lot of bad coincidences lately."

"You know," Nancy said quietly, "I do some private investigating back in River Heights. I might be able to help you find the cause of all this if you give me the details."

"We couldn't ask you to do that on your vacation," Kara answered, and Nancy watched the look of relief pass across Ned's face.

"But I suppose it wouldn't hurt to fill you in," Alex added, waving everyone into the office to sit down.

Nancy and Ned pulled chairs up to one of the two desks and sat down as Kara, who was holding Allison now, began to tell them what had been going on. "About a month ago strange things started happening to me on day trips. Ropes snapped under light conditions and crampons came loose," she explained.

"Did you say crampons?" Ned asked.

"Yes, the metal spikes that are attached to the bottom of your boots," Kara explained. "They give traction on the ice. Anyway, I thought the incidents were just bad luck, but now I'm not so sure." Allison squirmed off her mother's lap and ran back into the waiting room to play.

"On top of that," Alex put in, "this isn't the first break-in we've had. Just before we went on vacation, someone jimmied the lock on the front door, came in, but didn't take anything. I thought it was just a teenage prank. But now these incidents seem more serious. What do you think, Nancy?" he asked.

"I'm not sure," Nancy answered.

"Alex, could you hand me my cosmetics case?" Kara asked, pointing to the top desk drawer. "I could use some lip balm."

Alex pulled open the top drawer and handed Kara a small flowered pouch.

"Listen," Kara said, unzipping the case and pulling out a snakelike piece of paper. "We don't want to ruin your vacation, so let's not harp on this." She glanced down at the paper. "It could just be—"

Kara interrupted herself with a sharp cry. Her face went white as she handed the paper to Nancy.

> Things might look bad for Alpine
> Adventures, but they look a lot
> worse for you!

Chapter

Three

O H, NO," NANCY SAID, peering at the note in her hand. This definitely wasn't a prank.

"Are you all right?" Ned asked Kara as Alex put an arm around his wife after scooping up Allison, who had come to see if her mother was all right.

"I'm—I'm fine," Kara stammered, putting on a bright face for Allison. "It looks like these incidents aren't just bad luck after all."

"This is rapidly escalating into a serious problem," Alex said. "Nancy, will you take on our case? I know this is supposed to be your vacation,

21

but the police don't seem very concerned, and I'd never forgive myself if anything happened to Kara or Allie."

"Of course I will," Nancy answered, giving Ned a quick smile. She read the disappointment in his eyes, but he overrode that with a reassuring squeeze of her hand.

Nancy studied the note and considered the paper and handwriting. Unfortunately, the note was hand printed on regular notebook paper in plain block letters. Not much of a clue.

"Okay. What about suspects?" Nancy asked, getting down to business. "Do you have any enemies?"

"No," Kara answered. "Well, wait. Maybe I do." She turned to Alex, her eyes wide. "Do you think it could be Anne Bolle?"

"Anne Bolle," Alex repeated the name.

"Who is she?" Ned asked.

"A woman I used to climb with," Kara answered. "We were neck and neck on the climbing circuit for years. Then, about four years ago, she was disqualified in a rock-climbing competition for relying on the rope too much during a tricky move. I won the match—and the title of top female climber in the United States. Anne was furious and blamed me for her carelessness. She could never admit that it was her own mistake that cost her that match."

"Is she still on the climbing circuit?" Nancy inquired.

"Yes," Kara answered. "She's been doing very well since I stopped competing."

"So what would she have against you now?" Nancy wasn't sure she understood the connection.

"Well, the word is out that I'm getting back into competitive climbing," Kara explained.

"You are?" Ned interjected. "That's great."

"Where does Anne live?" Nancy asked, getting back to the issue at hand.

"In Utah, but she's in Washington now," Alex said. "We've asked her to come on the Rainier climb because she's so well known. And because she's a friend of Logan."

"It's not easy to get professional climbers to come on commercial trips. Their schedules are too hectic," Kara added.

"Where is Anne staying?" Nancy asked.

"With her friends Sarah and Joshua Jones in Seattle. She's been there about a month," Kara answered.

"When exactly did things start going wrong?"

"About three weeks ago," Alex said, suddenly understanding what Nancy was implying. "Do you think she's the culprit?" he asked excitedly.

"Possibly," Nancy said. "But it's only speculation. It takes solid proof to declare someone guilty of a crime. Have you seen her since she's arrived?"

"A few times," Kara answered. "And she's been super nice. She's always been so competitive—I can't imagine why she wants to be friends now."

Nancy was quiet for a minute, taking all of this in, but Alex interrupted her thoughts.

"Why don't we call it quits for now and head to the house for supper? It's been a long day."

"That sounds wonderful," Nancy said, suddenly realizing that she hadn't eaten anything all afternoon. She was famished.

An hour later Nancy and Ned were seated in the dining area of the Wheelers' house, which was wonderfully cozy and comfortable. A three-bedroom A-frame on the outskirts of town, the house afforded a view of the Cascade Mountains from the front, and the back was nestled into a grove of pine trees. It was decorated with country-style furniture, colorful throw rugs, and lovely watercolors on the walls.

"We try to eat as many complex carbohydrates as we can before a trip," Kara explained as she served whole-wheat pasta with a pesto primavera sauce for each of her guests.

"On Saturday you'll have a day of snow school," Alex told Nancy and Ned as he served the salad. "You'll learn about the equipment, falling techniques, and what to do in emergency situations."

"Emergencies?" Ned asked, concerned.

"When you're on a winter expedition, lots of unexpected things can happen," Kara explained. "But you're both in good shape and have basic climbing skills. You'll do fine."

"Oh, I wasn't worried," Ned said, forcing a smile. But Nancy could tell by the look in his handsome brown eyes that he was a little nervous about the whole adventure.

"How long will it take to get to the top?" Nancy asked, twirling pasta around her fork.

"It depends on the weather," Alex answered. "We're going up the southern side of the mountain, which is fairly well traveled, even in the winter. If all goes well, we'll spend two days hiking to base camp and then climb to the summit and back to base camp on the third day."

"Are you sure a couple of novices like us can handle it?" Ned asked.

"Of course," Alex replied. "Our trips don't require any technical experience. As long as you pass snow school and demonstrate that you're a team player, you'll do just fine."

"And standing on top of a fourteen-thousand-foot mountain is like nothing else in the world," Tsu added. "It's an incredible thrill."

"If you don't get blown off," Logan joked, bouncing Allison on his lap between bites. She giggled excitedly, hanging on tightly to his shirt.

"I'll be hanging on to you," Ned said, kidding.

"Then you'll be standing here in Enumclaw." Logan laughed. "I'm not going on the Rainier trip."

"You're not?" Nancy asked.

"No," he answered. "Too many guides and not enough novices," he joked. "Besides, somebody has to keep an eye on the office," he said.

There was no conversation for a few minutes while everyone ate.

"Bathtime," Alex said when they'd finished.

Allison slid off Logan's lap and reached for her dad's hand.

"Can Uncle Logan come?" Allison asked, raising her eyes to her dad's.

"Of course." Alex grinned. "We know he can't resist your bath toys." The threesome made their way down the hall to the bathroom.

While Nancy helped Kara clear the table and do the dishes, Tsu and Ned lit a fire in the living room. Then Kara served pie and coffee. Sitting next to Ned and sipping the warm beverage in front of the fire, Nancy relaxed for the first time since she'd arrived in Washington.

"So, why are you getting back into climbing?" Ned asked Kara.

"Now that Allie is three and in preschool, I have a little time for myself. I really miss climbing. I thought I'd stop missing it, but I miss it as much as ever—especially the solo ascents. There's nothing like standing on top of a twenty-thousand-foot mountain by yourself."

"You must be incredibly good," Ned murmured, and Nancy again saw the awe in his eyes.

"We'll see how I am after four years away from it," Kara answered.

Before long Alex and Logan had rejoined the

group and helped themselves to dessert. The group sat around the cozy fire, enjoying one another's company.

By ten o'clock, Nancy and Ned were exhausted. Kara had invited them to stay there, but Nancy insisted it would be better to go to a hotel.

Outside Nancy's door at the Park Center Hotel, Ned wrapped his arms around her and planted a soft, sure kiss on her lips. For a moment the world dropped away as their senses whirled. Then they pulled apart, and Nancy said good night and let herself into her room.

After flipping on the light, Nancy saw that the room was large and comfortable. Setting her duffel down on the suitcase rack, Nancy sighed. It had been a long day, and she was ready for a good night's sleep.

The next morning Nancy woke early and took a quick shower. After breakfast with Ned, she was eager to search through the ransacked mess at Alpine Adventures.

At the office Tsu was already at work trying to sort out the paperwork. Her hair was pulled back into a ponytail and the sleeves of her sweatshirt were pushed up to her elbows.

"Hi, guys," Tsu said. "Alex is in the equipment room with Logan. It looks like we're short some gear for the Rainier trip."

"Will the trip be canceled?" Nancy asked, concerned.

"Normally we'd postpone it, but we can't. *Great Outdoors* magazine wouldn't be too pleased to find out that their writer made the trip to Enumclaw for nothing," she said with a wry smile.

"I suppose," Nancy agreed. "But what will you do for equipment?"

"If there's a lot missing, Alex will make a trip to Tacoma to buy some things," Tsu replied.

"I think I'll go check out the gear," Ned murmured, giving Nancy a peck on the cheek. "Maybe I'll learn something," he whispered.

Nancy smiled, realizing that Ned was giving her an opportunity to talk to Tsu. She did want to ask some people a few questions, and Tsu was one of them. If she sifted through some of the papers at the same time, she might come up with a clue.

After Ned disappeared through the storage room doorway, Nancy asked, "How can I help?"

"If you could put the labeled piles into their files, it would be great," Tsu said, blowing a loose strand of hair out of her eyes. "I feel like I'm swimming in paper."

"I can see why," Nancy commented as she sat down on the floor. "What is all of this stuff?"

"Mostly trip information," Tsu said. "You know, different routes for climbs, route histories, information on the latest gear, and things like that."

Nancy glanced around, then picked up a pile of papers. "What's Cadaver Gap?" she asked, noticing the name on the top sheet of paper.

"It's a notorious gap between the Cowlitz and Ingraham glaciers on Mount Rainier," Tsu answered, making a face. "It's a pretty hairy area of the mountain."

"If the name means anything, I believe it," Nancy said as she began to skim an article. It was about all the accidents that had happened at Cadaver Gap—most of them fatal.

"Will you be coming on the trip?" Nancy asked, slipping the articles into their file and getting back to her questioning.

"Yeah." Tsu's face lit up. "It's going to be my last trip as an assistant guide. I've been working toward my certification for almost six months, and after this Wednesday I'll be a full guide."

"That's great," Nancy congratulated her. "Is that how long you've worked here, six months?"

"Yeah," Tsu replied. "But it seems like much less. I guess because I like it so much."

"Tsu," Nancy said. "Did anything suspicious happen the night of the break-in?"

"You know, I keep going over and over that night in my mind, but I always come back to the same idea—it was just like any other night."

Nancy believed her. Tsu didn't have any more clues about the ransacking than Nancy did.

Just then Alex came into the room. "I'm going to have to go to Tacoma to buy some new gear," he announced. "We just can't take this trip without new ropes and carabiners."

Picking up the phone, Alex dialed home and told Kara his plans. "I'll take your car since I already have it," he said. "I'll be home around three." He apologized to Nancy for not having more time to talk with her.

"Don't worry," Nancy responded, trying to hide her disappointment. "We'll have plenty of time to talk when you get back."

At twelve-thirty Nancy and Ned walked into The Kitchen, a comfortable café in Enumclaw that Logan had recommended. The smell of home-cooked breads and soups floated past Nancy's nostrils as she scanned the dining room for an empty booth.

Spotting one, she reached for Ned's hand and together they weaved past chatting customers and waitresses carrying huge metal trays filled with plates of food.

"Wow, what a place," Nancy commented as she slid into the booth. "I guess it's Enumclaw's hot spot for lunch."

"No kidding," Ned agreed with a grin. "If their sandwiches are half as good as they look, I'll be satisfied."

Nancy ordered a BLT and a bowl of minestrone. Ned requested the turkey club, and within a few minutes their food had arrived.

"So how was your talk with Tsu?" Ned asked, biting into his sandwich.

"Not so great. I mean, she's nice, but I don't think she knows anything. I want to find Anne Bolle. From what Kara tells me, she just might be my prime suspect."

"Right," Ned nodded. "But how can we track her down?"

Nancy gave Ned a sly grin, then concentrated again on the case. "Kara thinks she's staying in

Seattle—with some climbing friends named Joshua and Sarah Jones," Nancy said, dipping her spoon into the piping-hot soup. As she raised the spoon to her mouth, the conversation at the next booth caught her attention.

"I won't have that little know-it-all climber and his wife run us out of town. We were here first, and we'll get our business back on track—no matter what it takes!"

Chapter

Four

INSTINCTIVELY Nancy put a finger to her lips, signaling for Ned to be quiet. She turned her head so she could hear more of the conversation, but the two men had lowered their voices. Thinking fast, Nancy dropped her fork and gazed up at the men as she picked it up. One was fairly stocky, with gray hair and an unshaven face. He appeared to be in his midfifties. The other was younger, clean-cut, and of average build.

As Nancy sat up again, the waitress came by to ask if the food was all right.

"It's delicious," Ned responded.

When the waitress left, Nancy turned her head

to listen in on more of the men's conversation. When she didn't hear anything, she turned and saw that the two men were walking out the restaurant door.

"Shoot," Nancy murmured, exasperated. "I was hoping they'd stick around a little longer so I could hear a little more."

"I'm sure Alex or Kara will know who they are," Ned offered. "It sounded as if they're a competing company. How many other guide companies can there be in Enumclaw?"

"You're right," Nancy answered, sitting up straighter. "I'll ask Alex as soon as he gets back from Tacoma."

After finishing off their lunch with slices of pie, Nancy and Ned headed back to Alpine Adventures. There was no sign of life in the waiting room, but from the noise coming out of the office, Nancy guessed that Logan and Tsu were working there. As she approached the door, Nancy heard that they were in the middle of an intense discussion.

"There'll be lots of other trips," Logan was saying. "You'll have plenty of chances to get your certification. But when I take that new job, I'll be leaving for good. This is one of my last chances to climb with Alex and Kara."

"I know," Tsu agreed. "But I've worked hard for this, and getting my certification on the Rainier trip will make it special."

There were several moments of silence, then Logan spoke. "I didn't know it meant so much to you," he said, "or I wouldn't have asked."

"I know that it means a lot to you, too. But I really want to go," Tsu answered.

Realizing that the conversation was about to end, Nancy signaled for Ned to step away from the door quietly, then acted as if she had just come into the office. "Anybody here?" she called.

"We're back here," Logan called back.

"Oh, hi," Nancy said casually as she stuck her head into the office doorway. "We just came from lunch."

"The Kitchen has great food, Logan," Ned said as he leaned on the doorframe. "Thanks for recommending it."

"I'm glad you liked it," Logan answered with a smile. "It's one of my favorites."

Nancy stepped into the office. "Is Alex back yet?" she asked.

"No," Logan responded, checking his watch. "He said about three."

"Hmmm," Nancy said, pausing as Tsu excused herself and left the office. Nancy would have preferred to ask Alex about the men at the diner, since he knew about her investigation, but Logan would probably know who the men were, too. "Hey, Logan," she began, "could I ask you a question?"

"Sure," he answered. "What's up?"

"Does Alpine Adventures have any serious competition here in town?" she asked.

"Still thinking about Wednesday night's break-in, eh?" he responded. "I guess we've all got our theories as to who did it."

"I suppose we do," Nancy agreed. "Who do you think was responsible?"

"Hank Moody," Logan said, not hesitating for an instant.

"Who's Hank Moody?" Nancy asked, sliding into one of the two visitors' chairs across from the desk and unzipping her jacket.

"Oh, sorry," Logan said. "I'm not used to having to explain who people are. Hank Moody owns Outrageous Adventure, the other guide service in town."

"Really?" Nancy raised an eyebrow in interest.

"Yes," Logan continued. "Only his company is going down the tubes. Hank knows Rainier like the back of his hand, but that's the problem. He leads the same trips over and over, in exactly the same way. People don't want that. They want new experiences. A lot of his clients have come to us."

"So you think he could be responsible for the break-in?" Ned asked from the doorway.

Logan nodded. "He's the only person I know who has a motive."

"Does Alex know you feel this way?" Nancy asked.

"I told him last night," Logan answered. "But he doesn't think it's Moody."

"I guess you don't disagree very often," Nancy said.

"We usually see eye to eye on almost everything," Logan answered, a fondness in his voice. "We were roommates in college—and always said we'd go into business together when we graduated six years ago."

"It's great that it worked out," Ned put in.

"Well, it didn't work out at first," Logan responded. "When we got our diplomas, I became a mountaineer and Alex became a ski instructor. Then two years ago, Alex called and wanted to know if I'd help him open a guide service. Kara had had a baby the year before, and he needed someone to help him out for a while.

"I was on the U.S. climbing circuit, just starting to get sponsors to climb in Europe. But Alex talked me into it. He said we'd be just outside Rainier National Park. Rainier's the most respected mountain in the Lower Forty-eight, he said, and a volcano to boot. Alex had studied geology in college and has always had a thing for volcanoes. He'd even put in a bid on this office space. How could I refuse?"

"That was quite a sacrifice," Nancy commented.

"Not really." Logan shook his head. "I was ready for a break from heavy competition. Now that things have settled in here, I'm going back to climbing. I've just had an offer from Recreational Gear, a company that specializes in climbing equipment, to sponsor me, and I've accepted." Logan's face lit up with excitement as he spoke. "I'll be leaving in about a month."

Just then they heard the front door open and Tsu speak to someone. A man in his midtwenties poked his head in the office. He was fairly short, with olive skin, slicked back hair, and dark eyes.

"Can I help you?" Logan asked, getting up to assist him.

"We'll see," the man replied gruffly, pulling off his shearling gloves. "I'm Eladio Martinez, from *Great Outdoors* magazine."

Logan extended his hand to Eladio. "Of course, Eladio," he said. When Eladio shot him a nasty look, Logan added, "You don't mind if I call you Eladio, do you?"

"I suppose not." Eladio gave Logan and Nancy the once-over.

His piercing stare seemed to bore right through them, and Nancy felt an involuntary shiver. The man was giving her the creeps.

"I'm Logan Miller, Alex's right-hand man," Logan explained as Eladio turned back to him. "Alex had to make an unexpected trip to Tacoma to purchase some equipment, but we expect him back soon."

Eladio looked at his watch. "He asked me to come at three o'clock," he said. "And I don't appreciate it when people waste my time."

"I apologize, but we've had a bit of an emergency," Logan explained calmly. "If you'd like to wait—"

"I don't think so," he answered, and walked out. "Just be sure to tell Mr. Wheeler that *I* kept our appointment," he tossed back.

"Wow," Nancy commented when the main door closed behind him. "What a weirdo!"

They were still shaking their heads at the stranger's behavior when Kara burst through the front door, her face white.

"It's Alex," she cried. "He's been in a car accident!"

Chapter

Five

O H, NO," Tsu SAID in disbelief. "What happened?"

Kara took a deep breath. "The police called to tell me that he crashed on a mountain road near Buckley. The car was pretty crunched, but Alex wasn't badly injured."

"Where is he now?" Nancy questioned.

"At the emergency room at Buckley General Hospital," Kara answered. "Apparently he was hurt badly enough to need an exam. . . ."

"It's probably just routine," Ned said, a comforting arm around her shoulder.

"Ned's right," Logan put in. "I'm sure Alex is fine."

"Right," Kara said, trying to sound cheerful.

"Where's the car?" Nancy asked.

"They've towed it to a garage," Kara answered, pulling a piece of paper from her pocket. "Frank's Auto Body, on Route Four-ten."

"I'll call to check on the car," Nancy said. "So you won't have to worry about that."

"Great. I'm driving over to Buckley to pick up Alex," Kara continued. "Could you pick Allison up at preschool, Logan?"

"Of course," Logan answered.

"Would you like some company on the drive? I'd be happy to come with you," Ned offered Kara.

"That'd be great," Kara answered gratefully.

Ned gave Nancy a quick kiss goodbye. "Let's have dinner together at our hotel tonight," he said softly. "Just the two of us."

Nancy smiled and gave his muscular arm a light squeeze. "You're on," she responded warmly.

As the door closed behind Ned and Kara, Nancy went into action. She suspected that the car had been tampered with and wanted to ask the mechanic to check. She'd have to come up with some sort of cover, since she didn't have the authority to request that kind of information.

"Can I use the phone?" Nancy asked.

"Sure," Logan answered. "There's one in the back office."

"Thanks." Nancy went into the office to call. As the phone rang, she cleared her throat.

"Frank's Auto Body," said the voice on the other end of the line.

"Ah, yes," Nancy spoke confidently. "My name is Kara Wheeler. I'm calling about the red station wagon that was recently towed to your shop."

"It just came in," the man answered. "I haven't had a chance to really look at it yet, but I can tell you that it doesn't look good."

"Oh, that's terrible," Nancy said dramatically. Then she lowered her voice. "We just had that car serviced here in Enumclaw, at Busy Bee Auto," she confided. "And ever since then that car hasn't driven right. The mechanic insisted that the car was fine."

Sorry, Busy Bee, Nancy said to herself. She didn't like giving the auto shop a bad rap, but her little white lie was for a good cause.

44

"Not surprised," the man on the phone said.

"If you could keep an eye out for anything that Busy Bee might have done wrong, I'd really appreciate it," she finished.

"No problem, Mrs. Wheeler. I'll keep my eye out," the man said.

"Thank you, Mr. . . . um, I'm afraid I didn't catch your name," Nancy said.

"It's Joe," the man said. "I'm head mechanic here at Frank's."

"Thank you, Joe," Nancy said. "I'll call later to check on things."

"Fine, Mrs. Wheeler," he answered.

After hanging up Nancy went back into the front room, where Tsu and Logan were talking.

"I'd been telling Alex to get new tires put on Kara's car for weeks. The tires on the car now are really bald," Logan was saying.

That's right, Nancy mused. Alex took *Kara's* car to Tacoma. Added to the threatening note and her equipment problems, it looked like someone was out to get Kara, not Alpine Adventures.

Having done all the investigating possible at Alpine Adventures, Nancy wanted to head over to Outrageous Adventures and ask Hank Moody a few questions. "I'm going to run some errands," she said. "See you both later."

Nancy drove across town past a mixture of old and modern buildings, mostly all wood. The Outrageous Adventures office was in a small building at the end of a block, separate from the row of shops that lined the rest of the street. Taking a quick peek in the rearview mirror, Nancy smoothed her hair before walking up to the front door.

Stepping inside, Nancy was greeted by a woman in her midforties. "Can I help you?" the woman asked.

"Yes." Nancy smiled. "I'm looking for Mr. Hank Moody."

"Mr. Moody is in his office," the woman said, pointing to a door. "You can go on back," she said.

"Thank you." Nancy stepped through the doorway and saw the stocky, middle-aged man she had seen at The Kitchen earlier.

"Mr. Moody?" Nancy asked politely.

Hank Moody nodded, and Nancy continued. "I'm Nancy Drew, and I'd like to talk to you about Alpine Adventures."

At the mention of the company's name, Hank Moody stiffened slightly. "Of course," he responded smoothly. "I've heard they've had a run of bad luck lately." He gestured to a chair in front of his desk, and Nancy sat down.

"What exactly have you heard?" Nancy inquired.

"As I understand it, they've had a few minor falls on some local trips. And, of course, there was the break-in the other night. But why are you so interested in all of this?" he asked.

Nancy wasn't exactly thrilled to tell Hank Moody she was investigating the case, but she didn't see any way to put him off.

"Well, to tell you the truth, I'm a private investigator, and I'm trying to determine the cause for the accidents and the break-in," Nancy said. "The police believe that the break-in was just a teenage prank, but with the other mishaps I think there may be some foul play."

"In Enumclaw?" Hank Moody chuckled. "You're not from around here, are you? I'm sure that the occurrences over at Alpine Adventures are just coincidence, Miss Drew."

"I hope you're right, Mr. Moody," Nancy said, watching him closely for his reaction to her next question. "Where were you on Wednesday night?"

The muscles in Hank Moody's jaw tightened as he realized what Nancy was suggesting. "Are you saying that you think *I* broke into Alpine Adventures?" he bellowed. "I don't feel threatened by Alex Wheeler. I had my own guide service when he was in grade school! He's just a kid with fancy gear!"

"Where did you say you were?" Nancy repeated the question patiently.

"It's none of your business, but if you insist on knowing, I was at a Lions Club meeting until about ten o'clock. Afterward I went home to bed."

Nancy nodded. It would be easy enough to find out if Hank Moody was telling the truth.

"Well, thank you for your time," Nancy said graciously as she got up to leave. "I hope you understand that I'm only doing my job," she added.

"I suppose so," Hank answered gruffly. "But I hope you understand that I have better things to do with my time than pester Alpine Adventures."

Nancy walked back to her car in the cold, thinking. Hank Moody hadn't appreciated her accusation, but that didn't make him a guilty man. Sighing, Nancy started the car. Speculation wasn't going to solve her case.

While Nancy checked for messages at her hotel, she noticed a petite, athletic-looking woman standing at the check-in counter. Her long, honey-colored hair was pulled back from her pale face in a french braid, and her small mouth was curved down in a pout.

"What did you say your name was?" the receptionist was asking.

"Anne Bolle," the woman answered in a slightly annoyed tone. "I made the reservation yesterday."

Nancy's ears perked up when she heard Anne's name, and she smiled. Tracking down Anne Bolle was going to be easier than she'd thought.

"No messages for you, Ms. Drew," the attendant said.

"Thanks for checking." Nancy nodded, giving the man a sunny smile.

Out of the corner of her eye, Nancy saw the receptionist pull the key to Room 453 off its hook and hand it to Anne.

Up in her room, Nancy decided to finish unpacking. She still had a couple of hours before meeting Ned for dinner, which would give her time to pay Anne Bolle a visit. Just then the phone rang. The voice on the other end wasn't warm or friendly.

"Stay out of the problems at Alpine Adventures," said the hoarse, muffled voice. "Or I'll make sure that you do!"

Chapter

Six

NANCY CAUGHT HER BREATH as the phone line went dead. Someone wanted her off the case, but who knew she was on it? Hank Moody came to mind first. He could easily have followed her when she left Outrageous Adventures to find out where she was staying.

Well, if Hank Moody thought he could scare her off the case, he had another think coming.

Tossing her head defiantly, Nancy went back to unpacking. When the phone rang again a few minutes later, she hesitated a second before picking it up. It was Ned, calling to tell her that

Alex was fine. "We're bringing him home," Ned told her. "I should be back in time for dinner at eight."

"Fine," Nancy said. "Could you tell Kara that I've been in touch with the mechanic who has her car? I think someone may have tampered with it, and I used her name to get some information out of him."

"I'll let her know," Ned answered.

"Thanks, Ned. See you soon."

After hanging up, Nancy made a follow-up call to Joe at Frank's Auto Body.

"Your car sure was messed up, Mrs. Wheeler," Joe told Nancy. "The steering mechanism came loose. It wasn't attached to the wheels properly. That's why your husband ran off the road."

So someone did tamper with the car, Nancy thought. Now if she could just figure out who, she'd have made and solved the case. "That's terrible," Nancy exclaimed.

"The mechanic at Busy Bee should've seen it. When the car is up on the lift, it's pretty hard to miss something like that."

"What about the damage to the car?" Nancy asked, remembering that she was supposed to be Kara.

"The front end is pretty crunched and the

frame is bent," he answered. "I'd estimate the repairs at about two thousand."

Nancy gulped. Two thousand dollars! Alex and Kara weren't going to be happy about that. "I'll have to talk to my husband about this," Nancy said. "Can you hold off on the car until I call back tomorrow?"

"Sure thing," Joe said.

"You're next, Anne Bolle," Nancy said out loud as she picked up her room key from the dresser.

Nancy was on the fifth floor, so she took the stairs down to Anne's room. Knocking on the door, she arranged her face in a friendly expression.

The woman Nancy had seen in the lobby came to the door, her head wrapped in a towel, a thick terry cloth robe on.

"Are you Anne Bolle?" Nancy asked politely.

"Yes," the woman said reluctantly. She obviously didn't like to be disturbed.

"It's such a pleasure to meet you," Nancy said, and extended her hand. "You're my favorite climber."

Anne's face broke into a wide smile. "Thank you," she responded. "And you are?"

"Nancy Drew," she offered. "I'm a friend of

Alex and Kara Wheeler," she explained. "Could I please ask you a few questions about Alpine Adventures?"

"Well, I don't know what I can tell you," Anne answered, moving aside to let Nancy into her room. "But if you'll give me a few minutes to dress, I'll be happy to talk to you."

"Great," Nancy said, stepping into the room.

Anne gathered up a change of clothes and went into the bathroom, closing the door behind her.

"Perfect," Nancy murmured under her breath as she scoped out the room. Anne was obviously neat, because her things were in order.

Moving to one of the bedside tables, Nancy noticed a small leather organizer. It was lying open, and the corner of a lined piece of paper was sticking out. Picking it up, Nancy saw that it was a letter that Anne had started to someone named Jim. Probably a boyfriend, Nancy guessed. Nancy started skimming the letter. "Kara looks good for someone who hasn't climbed much in the past four years," Nancy read. "She might turn out to be something of a threat after all. . . ." Nancy was only halfway through the letter when she heard the bathroom door being opened. She stuffed the letter back where she found it, just before Anne came into the room.

"Much better," Anne said, tucking her turtleneck into her jeans. "Now, what did you want to talk to me about?"

"I just wanted to ask you a couple of questions about Alpine Adventures," Nancy said, seated in one of the brown swivel chairs. "I understand you're signed up for the Rainier trip."

"That's right," Anne confirmed. "Logan Miller asked if I'd be willing to go on the climb to give the company a bit of publicity. I agreed."

"Well, unfortunately, there have been a number of mishaps on the day trips that Alpine Adventures has led lately. And I'm sure you've heard about the break-in the other night."

"Break-in?" Anne's eyes grew wide. "I haven't heard about any break-in."

"Really?" Nancy said, surprised. "Enumclaw is such a small town, I would've thought everyone had heard about it."

"I've been away, staying with friends in Seattle," Anne explained. "I just arrived in Enumclaw."

"I see," Nancy said thoughtfully. "Well, someone broke into the Alpine Adventures office on Wednesday night. They trashed the files and stole a computer and several pieces of expensive gear."

"Oh, how awful," Anne said dramatically. "Do they know who did it?"

"The police think it was just a teenage prank," Nancy told her. "But in light of all the little accidents that have been happening, we're not so sure."

"Alex and Kara are both such nice people," she said in an overly sincere voice. "I can't imagine anyone hurting either of them."

"I know, Anne," Nancy said. "That's why I'm trying to get to the bottom of all this."

"Of course," Anne agreed.

"So I hope you won't mind if I ask you where you were on Wednesday night," Nancy said.

Anne's mouth dropped open slightly and her eyes narrowed. "Why would that be any of your business?" she challenged.

"It wouldn't, actually," Nancy admitted. "I'm just trying to prove that you're not a suspect. Some people think you might hold a grudge against Kara because of that competition four years ago," she said.

"A grudge?" Anne asked incredulously. "I assure you that I do not hold a grudge. Besides," she said, "Kara hasn't climbed in four years. She's no threat to me."

56

"I suppose she isn't," Nancy said out loud, while remembering what Anne had written in her letter.

"So, where did you say you were on Wednesday night?" Nancy asked.

"I didn't," Anne said coolly. "But if you really have to know, I was still with my friends in Seattle. We all went out for dinner that night."

"I see." Nancy nodded. *I can verify that with her friends if necessary,* she thought. Deciding that she had all the information she was going to get out of Anne Bolle, Nancy was ready to wrap up her interview.

"That's all I wanted to ask," Nancy said, getting up to go. "Thanks for taking the time to talk to me," she added.

"Certainly," Anne said, a bit sarcastically.

The woman seemed thoroughly annoyed, Nancy realized, but that wouldn't be unusual. The question was, was she up to no good?

Nancy walked back to her room, considering her interview. Anne was obviously lying about not being threatened by Kara, but she did have a supposed alibi for Wednesday night, which Nancy decided to check.

After picking up the phone, she dialed Directory Assistance to ask for Joshua Jones's phone number.

"Hello?" came a man's voice after a few rings.

"Yes, hello," Nancy said in an official-sounding voice. "I'm trying to reach Joshua Jones."

"This is he," the man said.

"Mr. Jones, my name is Mrs. Loomis. I'm with the Enumclaw Police Department, and I was wondering if you could help me with a routine procedure."

"I'd be happy to, if I can," Joshua said.

"Could you tell me," Nancy asked, "has Anne Bolle been staying with you?"

"Is she in some sort of trouble?" Joshua asked worriedly.

"No, no," Nancy assured him. "I'm just trying to confirm her whereabouts."

"Oh." Joshua sounded partly relieved. "Well, she was here until this afternoon, when she left for Enumclaw. Around three o'clock, I think."

"And was she with you on Wednesday evening?"

"Until about seven o'clock," Joshua confirmed. "We had a drink together, and then she went out."

"Did she tell you where she was going?" Nancy asked.

"No. I think she was meeting a friend for dinner," Joshua replied.

So she *was* lying, Nancy thought. "Good," she said into the phone, trying to sound casual. "That's what our records show."

"Is there anything else?" Joshua asked.

"No, that'll be all," Nancy replied. "Thank you for your help."

After hanging up the phone, Nancy sat down on her bed. Anne had lied. But why?

Nancy glanced at her watch. It was seven-fifteen. Just enough time to shower and get ready for dinner. She chose an emerald green knit dress, with jade beads, matching tights, and silver earrings.

At seven fifty-five Ned was at Nancy's door. "You look gorgeous," he murmured, wrapping his arms around her and planting a leisurely kiss on her lips.

"Thanks," Nancy said, enjoying the shiver she always felt whenever she and Ned were close.

"You're pretty slick yourself." Dressed in khakis, a black blazer, and colorful batik tie, Ned was especially handsome.

A few minutes later Nancy and Ned were seated at a cozy table in the corner of the restaurant. The white linen tablecloth glowed from the light of a flickering candle, and a vase held a small bouquet of carnations.

As they sipped their sodas, Nancy told Ned about her afternoon. "Hank Moody and Anne Bolle are my main suspects," Nancy explained, ready to continue.

"Nan," Ned said, leaning across the table and peering into her eyes. "Can we not talk about the case tonight? Please?"

Nancy bit her lower lip. The case was just beginning to take shape and she needed to talk things through. "I'll try," Nancy promised with a nod. "But there's so much happening, it won't be easy."

Just then the waiter brought their appetizers. While Nancy squeezed some fresh lemon onto her shrimp cocktail, Ned dipped his spoon into a crock of French onion soup, swirling a strand of melted cheese around it.

"Kara said that she's going to climb in the Northwestern Finals in March," Ned said excitedly. "Isn't that great?"

"Sure," Nancy said, dipping a shrimp into the cocktail sauce. She was pleased for Kara, but she wished Ned wasn't so excited about it.

"I think it's great that she's getting back into climbing," Ned went on. "A lot of women would give up that level of competition after having a baby. But she's committed to it."

"Ned," Nancy said slowly. "Let's not talk about Kara, either."

"Why not?" Ned asked, sounding offended.

"You spent most of the afternoon with her, and I'd just rather talk about something else," Nancy answered quietly.

"What's that supposed to mean?" Ned's voice was tight.

"You were awfully quick to offer to go with her to Buckley," Nancy said.

"She was upset, and I thought it would be a good idea for someone to ride with her," Ned said hotly.

"Well, I'm glad I had the case to work on, so you could offer your services," Nancy shot back before she had a chance to think about what she was saying.

"I don't want to listen to this, Nancy," Ned said, pushing his chair back from the table. He stood up, throwing his napkin over his soup bowl. "And to tell you the truth, I've lost my appetite!"

Chapter

Seven

NANCY WAS TOO SURPRISED to speak as she watched Ned leave the dining room. What had happened? Calling the waiter over, she asked him to put the check on her room tab. Then she went back to her room to get a jacket and hat. She needed to think things through, and a walk in the cold night air seemed the best solution.

Outside, Nancy slowly made her way down a quiet street. How could Ned be so insensitive? she asked herself. Why did he get so defensive when Nancy said she didn't want to talk about Kara? It was a reasonable request, especially after his.

Nancy sighed, finally reasoning herself to an understanding of Ned's point of view. They had planned a romantic dinner, and Nancy had immediately talked about her case. Of course Ned was feeling frustrated.

As for Kara, Ned really was just trying to help her. He loves me, Nancy thought, and I've got to trust him.

Nancy saw that she and Ned had misunderstood each other. He deserved an apology, she knew. Feeling better, she headed back to the hotel.

Nancy found Ned in the lounge. "Hi," she said softly.

Ned smiled shyly. "Hi to you, too," he said.

"I just wanted to tell you that I'm sorry," Nancy began, twisting her beads around her finger. "I didn't mean to accuse you of wanting to be with Kara more than me."

"Oh, Nan." Ned's voice was full of tenderness as he reached for Nancy's hand. "You're the only girl for me." He smiled, and Nancy's heart melted. "And I'm sorry, too," he continued. "I know you're trying to solve this case, and it didn't help when I refused to listen. I'll try to be more considerate."

Nancy's heart soared. This was the Ned she loved, the caring, sensitive Ned. "I promise as soon as this case is over, we'll do something special for just us," she vowed.

Ned stood and held Nancy close. They peered into each other's eyes for a moment, and their lips met in a quick, sweet kiss. Arms around each other, they marched off to the elevator, enjoying the warmth of being close.

The next morning Nancy and Ned grabbed some muffins and coffee from the breakfast buffet and drove to Alpine Adventures. Dressed in layers, they were ready for a day of grueling snow school.

"I hope this gorgeous weather holds," Nancy commented.

"I do, too," Ned agreed as he drove the car into the parking lot.

Inside, Alex and Kara were preparing the gear for the day.

"How are you feeling?" Nancy asked Alex as she and Ned took off their gloves and unzipped their parkas.

"Fine," he said, and Nancy was relieved that he was in good spirits. She only hoped that her news wouldn't change that too much. "I'm just a little stiff."

"What did the mechanic tell you?" Kara asked Nancy, her voice full of concern.

"His estimate for repairing the vehicle is two thousand dollars," Nancy answered slowly.

Alex groaned. "That's what I was afraid of," he said. "But our insurance will cover most of it."

"There's something else," Nancy said. "It looks like someone tampered with the steering mechanism on your car."

Kara put a hand on her husband's arm in alarm. "You mean, on purpose?" she asked.

"Exactly. Apparently someone loosened the tie rods between the wheels and steering mechanism. I think you have to tell the police," Nancy added.

The color drained from Alex's face. "I'd like to avoid that at all costs," he said firmly. "Our reputation is already on the line, and this trip is important."

"All right," Nancy agreed reluctantly. "We won't report anything—for now."

"Thanks," Kara said sincerely.

"I need to ask one more thing," Nancy said. "Was there a Lions Club meeting last Wednesday?"

"Yes," Alex replied, without hesitating. "They meet every Wednesday at the town hall."

"And do you happen to know if Hank Moody goes to those meetings?" Nancy questioned.

"He does." Alex said, nodding. "He's the club treasurer."

Then I guess his alibi holds, Nancy thought as the door opened and Eladio, Anne, and Tsu came in.

Decked out in his alpine gear, Eladio didn't look quite so creepy, and Nancy noticed that he wasn't as rude to Alex as he had been to Logan the day before.

Although Anne was a professional climber and didn't need any climbing instruction, she was at snow school to get to know the group better. She greeted Nancy stiffly, and again Nancy wondered what she was hiding.

Another young woman, Lisa Osterman, had signed up for the trip at the last minute. Lisa was of average height, with auburn hair and hazel eyes. She seemed nervous as she waited to get her gear. Nancy wondered where she was from and if she was an experienced climber.

Each person was given the necessary gear, including an ice ax, a harness, goggles, crash helmets, and crampons.

"These look dangerous," Lisa commented as she squinted at a crampon. It was a metal frame with nylon straps and twelve sharp metal spikes protruding downward.

"They give you traction on the ice," Kara explained. "I guarantee you'll be glad to have them on the mountain."

"Will they hurt my boots?" Lisa asked.

"Of course not," Kara said with a smile. "They're designed to work with boots."

Just then, Logan arrived to watch over the office. When all the climbers had their gear together, the group piled into the van for the drive to Mt. Rainier National Park.

"The point of snow school is to learn how to go into crampon-and-ice-ax arrest, which means stopping yourself if you start to fall," Tsu told the group as the van turned onto a snow-covered road. "We'll also show you how to pressure-breathe, which helps eliminate altitude sickness. I realize that for some of you this will be old hat," Tsu continued. "But it's also a good chance for us to learn to work together as a group."

"This is so exciting," Nancy whispered to Ned, who was sitting beside her. Ned put an arm around her, giving her a squeeze. "I can't wait to get out there and give this falling stuff a shot."

"I'm sure you'll put me to shame," Ned answered, laughing.

A few minutes later the van pulled into a small parking lot and the group climbed out. Everyone put on crampons before beginning to hike up a moderate slope lined with towering firs. The sky was bright and clear and the air was crisp and cold.

"We're going to follow the Carbon River for a while and then hike up onto the lower sections of Mother Mountain," Kara explained as the line of hikers made their way up beside the winding, snow-covered river.

"When you pressure-breathe," she continued, "exhale forcefully, but slowly." She took a breath and made a *phhhhshhhhh* sound as she let the air out. "It sounds weird, but it really helps your body adjust to the altitude. Down here it's not necessary. But once we get past seven thousand feet or so, it will be really important."

Nancy and the others practiced the breathing. The only trouble was that the breathing made it difficult to hear what the others were saying. Nancy was hoping to get a handle on Eladio and pick up more information about Anne and Lisa. She took a few quick steps forward to try to listen in on a conversation between Lisa and Kara.

"I climbed the Latok last summer," Nancy overheard Lisa telling Kara. "You know, in Nepal."

"You mean Pakistan," Kara answered naturally.

"Of course," Lisa muttered, embarrassed. "That's what I meant. I always get that mountain confused with the Unnamed Tower."

"It's the Nameless Tower," Kara corrected. "And it's in Pakistan, too."

"Right, well, anyway," Lisa stammered, "it was so difficult I almost didn't make it."

Lisa sounded like she was trying to impress Kara, but she constantly put her foot in her mouth! She didn't sound as knowledgeable about mountaineering as she pretended.

After about forty minutes of hiking, the group came to a fairly steep slope. "This is it," Kara said, putting her climbing rope down on the ground. "We're all going to practice climbing up to that ridge, falling as we go." She pointed to a ledge about forty feet above where they were standing.

"I just hope all of this falling doesn't hurt my parka," Eladio commented.

"For the first part of this class you won't be attached to a rope," Kara continued. "It's not that steep, and we want each of you to get used to the feel of falling. But when we reach ten thousand feet on Rainier, we'll be roped together in two groups."

"When you feel yourself slip," Tsu said, "hold your ice ax in one hand, with the sharp end facing out. I'll demonstrate." She took about ten steps forward, holding her ice ax in a ready position as she moved up the slope.

"When you fall," she went on, "you should always shout 'Falling,' so the people around you know what's happening. I'll demonstrate."

Tsu took a few more steps forward, then pushed her arms and legs out from under her. "Falling!" she shouted as she went into a spread-eagle position and jammed her ice ax and crampons into the icy slope.

"Who wants to go first?" Kara asked when Tsu stood up again.

"I will." Anne stepped forward. She walked several feet up the slope, then did a graceful spread eagle, calling out, "Falling."

"Notice the way Anne dug her crampons into the ice at an angle," Kara said. "That's the best way to get traction."

"Who'd like to go next?" Kara asked.

Nobody responded.

"Nancy?" Kara asked. "What about you?"

"Sure." A shot of adrenaline pulsed through Nancy as she stepped forward, her ice ax in position for a fall. She began walking up the slope. "Here goes," she muttered under her breath. "Falling," she shouted, pulling her crampons out of the ice and letting herself slide down the slope. Her body slammed against the hard ice, but soon she was able to force her arms and legs into a spread-eagle position and dig her ice ax and crampons into the ice. In a matter of seconds she had stopped herself.

"Nice job," Tsu said.

Nancy smiled, feeling her heart rate drop back to almost normal. "Thanks."

Nancy watched while the rest of the group practiced falling. Eladio had a hard time because he was too worried about his new parka.

"I hope he doesn't fall on the trip," Ned whispered to Nancy.

Lisa obviously knows what she's doing, Nancy thought as she watched the young woman take a fourth practice fall. She was always able to get her ice ax into the snow quickly, but she sounded frantic as she shouted, "Falling."

"Looking good," Kara congratulated the group after about an hour and a half of hard practice.

"Now we're going to climb up to that ledge so that we can show you some rescue procedures."

"Rescue?" Eladio asked, sounding nervous.

"It's just routine," Tsu assured him. "We take every precaution on the mountain. But if anything were to happen, we want everyone to be prepared."

After several minutes of relatively easy climbing, the group reached the ledge. "The first thing we're going to do is a mock crevasse rescue. A crevasse is a giant crack in a glacier—sometimes they're hundreds of feet deep," Tsu explained. "We'll pretend that this ledge is a crevasse and that someone has fallen in," she finished.

Nancy carefully leaned over the edge and saw that the drop from the ledge was about a hundred feet, but it wasn't a ninety-degree drop.

"I'll play the victim," Kara announced. "And everyone else, watch carefully."

"Actually, why don't I do it? I'd like the practice," Tsu responded. "You can work with the group, Kara."

Kara nodded as Tsu began to pound a three-foot stake into the ice. "This is a picket anchor," Tsu explained as she worked. "It's one of the few pieces of equipment that can really anchor a person to a slope."

Once the anchor was pounded into the ice, Tsu tied the rope around it, then stepped into a special climbing harness and tied the other end of the rope into the harness. She began to ease herself down the steep slope.

"Now, if Tsu had actually fallen, everyone on her rope would immediately go into a spread-eagle arrest," Kara told the group. "That's important, because your combined weight will keep her from falling too far. Once Tsu is safe, the person at the back of the—"

A sudden scream stopped Kara short. Nancy leaned over the edge of the ledge and watched in horror as Tsu careened down the slope!

Chapter

Eight

NANCY SAW that the rope that had safely anchored Tsu to the ledge had snapped in two, and one end dangled lazily across the ice. As Tsu tumbled downward, she tried to get into a spread-eagle position to do an arrest, but she was falling so fast it was impossible.

After about ten awful seconds, Tsu spread her arms and legs and dug her crampons and ice ax into the snow.

"Are you all right?" Kara called down.

"I think so," Tsu replied shakily. She clung to the icy mountainside with her ice ax and crampons. The slope was too steep for her to ease her way to the bottom. Tsu needed help.

Kara took control of the situation. "Okay," she said. "We need to get down to Tsu as quickly, and as safely, as we can."

"Kara," Anne interjected, "let me rappel down to her? I could then help her to the bottom. That way you and the others can climb down the way you came up. It will be safer for everyone."

Kara thought for a second, then smiled gratefully. "You wouldn't mind?" she asked.

"Of course not," Anne answered.

Nancy realized that Anne's concern for Tsu was genuine—she was willing to take a risk to help Tsu so that Kara could stay with the group.

Within minutes Anne was standing at the edge of the ledge. She pulled on the rope to make sure it was still securely tied to the anchor. Then she fed it through a piece of metal equipment called a figure eight. The friction from the tight fit would keep Anne from descending too fast. Finally she put on a harness and looped the rope through it, tying it tightly.

Lightly holding the section of rope that was closest to the anchor, Anne let the rope slide through her glove. At the same time, she dug her crampons into the ice and "walked" backward down the mountain. She held her right hand at her side and fed the long section of rope through the figure eight, using both the tension of the rope on the figure eight and the anchor for support.

Before long she reached Tsu. Tying Tsu's broken rope into her own harness, Anne helped her to the bottom of the slope.

With Tsu safely off the ice, Kara untied the rope from the anchor, then pulled the anchor out of the ice. The group then carefully walked back down the other side of the ledge.

"Are you all right?" Nancy asked Tsu when they got to her.

"I'm fine," she answered, wincing. "But I don't think my shoulder is doing so well."

Nancy took her gloves off and ran her fingers lightly along Tsu's shoulder. "It feels like it might be dislocated," she said. "We'll have to get you to the hospital right away."

Leaning over, Nancy looked at the frayed rope that had caused Tsu's accident. "Did you notice anything wrong with this rope before the climb?" she asked.

"No," Tsu answered. "All of the gear was fine when I checked it last night."

This looks like another case of sabotage aimed at Kara, Nancy thought, remembering that Kara was to play the victim.

Since all of the necessary climbing skills had been covered, Kara and Alex called it a day for snow school.

Tsu went to the emergency room and Anne offered to stay with her.

When the rest of the group finally returned to Alpine Adventures, it was nearly dinnertime. Nancy and Ned had just enough time to shower and change before the pre-trip dinner at the Loading Dock, a family-style restaurant in town.

"Do you think you could give me a ride back to the hotel?" Lisa asked Nancy and Ned. "I didn't rent a car, since I'll only be here for a few days."

"Sure," Nancy responded. This would be a perfect opportunity to question Lisa, she thought.

"Where have you climbed, Lisa?" Nancy asked nonchalantly as Ned drove.

"In Europe and the Far East," Lisa answered, gazing out the car window. "You know, the Alps, the Himalayas."

"Right," Nancy said. But she remembered that Lisa had messed up the names and locations of

Himalayan peaks during her conversation with Kara.

"I hope the food at the Loading Dock is good," Ned said, changing the subject. "I'm starved."

"It's one of the best restaurants in town," Lisa answered. "They serve a terrific roast chicken."

"You've been there?" Nancy asked, surprised. "I didn't know you'd visited Enumclaw before."

"Oh, I haven't," Lisa stammered, nervously fiddling with the end of her seat belt strap. "I've just heard good things about it."

"Oh, I see," Nancy murmured, not believing Lisa for a minute. Lisa Osterman was hiding something, and Nancy intended to find out what.

Nancy called Ned from her room and arranged to meet him in fifteen minutes to search Lisa's room together.

As she stood under the spray of a hot shower, Nancy considered the events of the day. Anne Bolle's reaction to Tsu's fall had convinced Nancy that there was a good side to the woman, but that didn't mean she wasn't out to get Kara. And Lisa Osterman wanted Nancy to believe that she was a stranger to Enumclaw, yet she knew at least a little about the town. Could she be a suspect? Nancy wondered.

After toweling off, Nancy slipped into black wool trousers and a kelly green sweater. She gave her thick reddish blond hair a few quick strokes with the hairbrush, and added a touch of natural lip balm.

Nancy dialed Lisa's room number. There was no answer, which meant the young woman had already left for dinner.

A few minutes later Nancy was picking the lock to Lisa's room while Ned kept a lookout. Slipping inside, Nancy switched on the light.

Piles of clothes were scattered on the floor and drawers hung open with more clothes spilling out. Her dresser was scattered with crumpled pieces of paper and various cosmetics.

"Wow, is she messy," Ned commented. "How do you suppose she finds anything?"

"She's probably used to it," Nancy answered, laughing softly.

After picking up Lisa's address book, Nancy found a scrap of paper with Alpine Adventures' address and telephone number on it. It wasn't anything incriminating, but she stuffed it into her pocket anyway.

Turning toward the closet, Nancy began to sift through Lisa's clothes while Ned riffled through the bedside table drawers.

Nancy next sifted through the trash can, but her search turned up only an empty soda can and some crumpled napkins. Discouraged, Nancy moved to the table by the window.

"Hey, Nan, look at this," Ned called from Lisa's dresser. He was holding an airline ticket.

"It's dated two weeks ago," Nancy commented out loud. "She's been in Enumclaw for two weeks. I *thought* she was hiding something."

Pulling a pen and pad of paper out of her purse, Nancy quickly jotted down the Pacific Airlines flight information on the ticket, as well as the date of issue. Just as she was closing her notebook, she heard footsteps moving down the hall. The footsteps then stopped right outside the room. Nancy's eyes grew large as a key was slipped into the lock and the doorknob began to turn.

Nancy and Ned were trapped!

Chapter

Nine

As THE DOORKNOB continued to turn, Nancy
slid the plane ticket back onto the dresser, and
Ned and she ducked behind the bed. At the exact
moment they disappeared out of sight, the door
to the hotel room opened.

Nancy's heart pounded hard inside her chest.
Had Lisa seen them? Was anything noticeably
out of order? She was grateful that Lisa wasn't a
neatnik.

It seemed forever before Lisa retrieved whatever it was she'd come to fetch. No sooner was
she out the door than the phone rang.

"What now?" Lisa grumbled as her footsteps came back toward the bedside table.

Thank goodness the phone was on the opposite side of the bed, Nancy thought, or they'd have been discovered. Her nerves were thoroughly on edge.

"Hello," Lisa said, sounding anxious and irritated. "Yes, it's me," she continued. "Who else would it be? Don't worry, I'll take care of it."

There were a few moments of silence as the person on the other end of the phone spoke.

"I have to go, or I'll be late," Nancy heard Lisa say finally. "I'll call as soon as I have some news." A moment later Lisa put the phone down and walked toward the door. She flipped the lights off. When Lisa closed the door, Nancy and Ned finally relaxed.

"That was too close," Ned said, standing up and brushing off his pants.

"No kidding," Nancy agreed, turning one light back on.

"Who do you suppose she was talking to?" Ned asked.

"I don't know," Nancy answered. "But I've got a hunch it's got something to do with this case."

After a last-minute check to be sure everything

was as they had found it, Nancy turned out the light. Within fifteen minutes they'd arrived at the Loading Dock, where Alex had reserved a small room off the main dining area for the group.

Nancy and Ned were the last to arrive. Anne, Lisa, Eladio, and Tsu were already seated at the long, rectangular table, and Alex and Kara were arranging handouts on a small side table.

"How are you feeling?" Ned asked Tsu as he and Nancy approached the table.

"Not too bad," Tsu answered, but Nancy noticed the pain in Tsu's eyes. "The bad part is that I won't be able to climb Rainier tomorrow," Tsu added softly.

Of course, Nancy thought to herself. Tsu had been looking forward to getting her certification, and now that had been put on hold.

"I'm so sorry," Nancy said.

Tsu sighed. "There'll be other climbs, I know," Tsu answered. "I just have to be patient."

Scanning the table, Nancy saw that Lisa was next to Eladio near one end. She sat close to Lisa to keep an eye on her. Ned chose a seat across from Nancy.

Dinner was delicious. A salad of mixed greens was served with a wonderful blue cheese dressing, followed by a hearty vegetable soup. The main course was pasta with a red pepper and shrimp sauce, accompanied by crusty whole-grain bread.

Eladio chatted with Alex about a new line of climbing ropes. Alex was nodding, pretending to listen intently, but Nancy guessed he was only being polite. It wouldn't do him any good to offend a man who'd soon be writing an article about his company.

While Kara cut Allison's pasta into bite-size pieces, she and Anne talked about past climbing competitions. Kara seemed to be enjoying the conversation. In fact, the two women even laughed together over a shared joke.

Maybe they're no longer enemies, Nancy mused, but she wasn't sure. Anne *had* gone out of her way on the climb to help Kara in a difficult situation, but that wasn't proof the woman wouldn't try to hurt Kara still.

Logan was telling Ned about Tsu's first winter climb on Rainier. "She was amazing," he said. "Didn't get any altitude sickness and climbed faster than I did. The woman is a natural." Tsu smiled at Logan, but Nancy sensed the kind words weren't making her feel better. No matter how good a climber Tsu was, she wouldn't be climbing Rainier tomorrow.

"I always get terrible altitude sickness," Lisa chimed in. "I pressure-breathe like crazy, but it never seems to do much good." Nancy watched Lisa's face as she spoke. It was virtually the first thing she'd said during dinner. Nancy felt that Lisa was a prime suspect, but she needed proof, and so far she wasn't getting any.

After three-berry pie and ice cream, Alex and Kara gave each person a handout that described the route the group would be taking up the mountain. They'd climb the mountain from the south, starting at the National Park Service lodge at Paradise.

"We'll go over climbing procedure when we hike in tomorrow," Kara said. "But it's important to understand that Rainier is a big mountain with power all its own. We know the mountain, and as your guides it's our responsibility to make sure we all make it safely to the top. The most important aspect of this is to work together as a team, just as we did today when Tsu fell."

"The first day will be just a few hours of easy snowshoeing," Alex said. "Day two will be longer, but not much more difficult. The real work will come on day three, when we'll spend six to ten hours on the move, some of it in darkness."

"We won't be doing any technical climbing

with ropes and rappelling," Kara said. "Getting to the top of Rainier only requires hiking and snowshoeing. But the mountain has many crevasses and snow bridges, which make it tricky. We know where these crevasses and bridges are and can navigate the mountain. But what you need to do is stay alert. . . ."

"This trip isn't about getting to the top as fast as we can," Alex added. "It's about the magic of Rainier and the experience of climbing it. It's an incredible mountain, and not everybody can make it to the top."

As Nancy listened to Alex and Kara speak, her pulse raced. She and Ned had come out West to go skiing, and instead they were setting out to climb one of North America's best-known mountains. She just hoped that none of them would be in danger on the climb.

When the meeting was over, Nancy asked Ned to wait for her while she went to the rest room.

Kara was washing her hands when Nancy went in. "You and Anne looked like you were having a nice time," Nancy commented.

"We were," Kara answered, reaching for a towel to dry her hands. "And I wanted to tell you that I was wrong in suspecting she was responsible for the threats and the break-in."

And all of the accidents, Nancy thought to herself.

"After Anne and Tsu got back from the emergency room," Kara continued, "Anne and I had a good talk. She apologized for being so nasty to me when we were competing. She said that her obsession to win had made her blind to her own mistakes. I think she was being sincere, Nancy," Kara said solemnly. "And I don't think she'd do those horrible things."

"I'm glad you're getting along better," Nancy said, knowing she had to tell her that Anne could still be a suspect. "She could still be up to no good."

Kara's eyes widened. "I don't think so," she said earnestly.

"I hope you're right," Nancy said, "but we have to be careful."

Kara nodded. "I know," she said softly.

"Listen," Nancy said, changing the subject. "I need to talk to you and Alex about the case. Can we meet in the dining room for a few minutes?"

"Sure," Kara answered. "I just need to take care of a couple of things first."

A few minutes later Nancy walked back into the dining room. Allie was quietly playing with a puzzle in the corner. Logan and Alex talked beside her. Sensing that the two men were discussing something serious, Nancy approached them until she was within earshot, then pretended to tie her shoe while she listened to their conversation.

"With everything that's been going on, I really need you to stay behind and keep an eye on the office," Alex was saying.

"Tsu can watch the office," Logan said, so quietly Nancy had to strain to hear.

"I don't think that's a good idea," Alex answered. "She's been through a lot, and I think she needs time to rest her shoulder."

"But you need another guide on this trip, and it should be me." Logan paused for a moment as Nancy straightened up. "And if you won't let me go," he continued, "then maybe I should tell Recreational Gear that I'm available to start the European circuit immediately."

Chapter

Ten

WOW, NANCY THOUGHT as she moved closer to the men, pretending to look for something she had left behind. Logan really wants to take this trip. She couldn't blame him. He had worked hard to make it all come together.

Alex's eyebrows were knit tightly together. "It doesn't need to come to that, Logan," Alex answered steadily. "I'm sure we can work something out. It's just that I don't want to ask Tsu to watch the office by herself, since she's been injured. With all the strange things that have been going on, I think it would be asking too much."

"I disagree," Logan replied. "She's feeling blue since she can't climb, so feeling useful would be good medicine."

Alex considered for a minute, then nodded. "You could be right," he said thoughtfully. "I'll ask her how she feels. If it's all right with her, it's all right with me."

"Great." Logan smiled at his friend. "I'll go find her so we can settle this now."

As Logan left the room, Nancy approached Alex. "Delicious dinner," she said.

Alex smiled, but Nancy could see the strain on his face. The break-in and accidents were taking their toll. "I wanted to update you on the case," she said.

"My investigation has turned up a new suspect," Nancy began as Kara joined them. "And an interesting one at that."

Alex and Kara stood perfectly still as they waited for Nancy to go on.

"What do you know about Lisa Osterman?" Nancy asked pointedly.

"Lisa's a suspect?" Kara didn't conceal the surprise in her voice. "But she just got into town a couple days ago."

"I searched her hotel room, and found an

airline ticket that shows she arrived in Tacoma over two weeks ago."

"Really," Kara said.

"But she could have stayed in Tacoma for a while before coming here," Alex pointed out.

"True," Nancy admitted. Was her suspicion of Lisa unfounded? "But my intuition tells me she's hiding something. Has she said anything to you that's unusual?"

"Just the way she mixed up the names and locations of peaks in Pakistan. I kind of doubt that she's done much climbing in the Himalayas, no matter what she says," Kara said.

Just then Logan and Tsu came into the dining room, and judging from the gleam in Logan's eye, Nancy guessed that Tsu was willing to run the office alone.

"I don't mind taking care of the office, Alex," Tsu said, her face brightening a bit. "It will give me something to think about other than myself while my shoulder heals."

"All right then, it's settled." Alex grinned. "Logan, do you have time to go as a guide?"

Logan laughed. "I think I can fit it into my busy schedule," he said. "But I'd better get home and start packing." He and Tsu said good night and left together.

"We have to consider the possibility that Lisa may be responsible for everything that's happened," Nancy said, getting back to the subject of Lisa.

"Then I want her off the trip," Alex said firmly.

"But, Alex, we aren't positive it's her," Kara countered. "And she's already paid for the trip and gone through snow school. We can't just tell her she's out."

"I have to agree with Kara," Nancy put in. "Of course, there's still Hank Moody as a suspect. So we don't know anything for sure."

Alex hesitated for a moment, then nodded slowly. "I suppose it would be foolish of her to try to pull something with all of us on the trip," he said. "We'll let her come, but let's keep an eye on her at all times."

"All in a day's work," Nancy joked, then signaled to Ned that she wanted to leave.

"Listen," Nancy said as Ned folded up the newspaper he'd been reading and slipped it under his arm, "I want to head over to Outrageous Adventures to see if I can dig up anything on Hank Moody."

"I'm game," Ned responded. "Let's go."

"Do you want me to come in with you?" Ned asked in the car outside the dark office building.

"I could use your help searching," Nancy answered, "but on second thought, it would be better if you stayed outside to keep watch."

"Okay, gorgeous," Ned answered, leaning over and planting a soft, lingering kiss on her lips. "Are you sure you don't want to keep watch with me?" he asked when they had pulled apart, his brown eyes twinkling with mischief.

"Ned Nickerson," Nancy said, swatting him on the arm playfully. "Are you trying to keep me from my case?"

"Of course not," he said, "but with the chilly winter air blowing outside, I can't help but wish you could stay here and keep me warm."

"I'll be back soon," Nancy promised, and gave Ned one last peck before slipping out of the car quietly to pick the front lock.

Since the front office had no windows, the room was pitch black. Nancy slipped her lock-picking tools back into her coat pocket and pulled a penlight out of her purse. A second later the beam lit up the room.

Nancy moved toward Hank's office, where she took off her coat and went through his desk drawers. It was filled with papers and business envelopes, but Nancy found nothing of interest.

Nancy noticed a stack of papers on top of the desk and began to sift through them. A recent credit card bill had a charge of three hundred and fifty dollars to Pacific Airlines—the airline that Lisa had flown to Tacoma!

Nancy checked the date of the bill, and saw that the transaction took place the same day Lisa's ticket was issued! Had Hank Moody bought Lisa's ticket? Was she working for him? Nancy wondered as she pulled a pen out of her purse and jotted down the credit card information.

Nancy moved toward the small table near the window with pictures of Hank's family. The first photo showed a much younger Hank. He was on top of a mountain, smiling at the camera with a young, attractive woman by his side. Probably his wife, Nancy guessed.

After scanning the next photograph, Nancy knew it had been taken a good many years earlier. There were lots of smiling faces in the picture, and Nancy recognized the woman from the other photo standing near Hank. One of the children in the picture seemed familiar, but Nancy couldn't place her.

After putting the second photo down, Nancy

went back through the reception area to look for the gear room. The third door she opened into a room with the musty smell of camping gear.

Nancy slowly made her way down one aisle. She wasn't exactly sure what to look for, except possibly a lot of fancy-looking gear with the Alpine Adventures name stitched into it. She passed the backpacks and the sleeping bags and made her way back toward the door along an aisle with cookware, stoves, and water filters.

When she turned down the third aisle, she found stacks of crampons, ice axes, and harnesses. Picking up a crampon, she noted that it was different from those used at Alpine Adventures. It had an old leather strap and the teeth were a different shape. Running her finger along the sharp edge of the teeth, she noticed that they weren't all that sharp.

"I guess Hank isn't using state-of-the-art equipment these days," Nancy murmured as she put the crampon down and moved toward the ice axes. Just as she picked one up, she heard a shuffling sound behind her.

Startled, Nancy whirled around, but in doing so lost her grip on her penlight. As it fell to the floor it cast a drunken light pattern on the wall and then went out.

Nancy groped for the light, but before she could grasp it, she heard footsteps in the darkness. A second later she heard the decisive slam of a door.

Nancy had been locked in.

Chapter

Eleven

Nancy waited in the darkness, listening to the footsteps fade away and focusing on a way to get out.

Feeling along the cold cement floor, Nancy finally found her penlight. As she guessed, it no longer worked. The fall to the floor had smashed the bulb.

Nancy cautiously moved toward the door, feeling along the walls and shelves. When she reached the door, her suspicions were confirmed —she was locked in.

Nancy unzipped her purse and began to search for the tool she used to pick locks. It wasn't there.

With a sinking feeling, Nancy realized that she had slipped it into her coat pocket and left her coat in Hank Moody's office.

Nancy turned around and squinted into the darkness. She had to find something to jimmy the lock. But there was no window in the gear room and she couldn't see a thing.

Slowly and carefully, Nancy began to make her way down the aisle to the cooking utensils. Suddenly, she tripped and fell to the floor, knocking her head hard against a shelf. She groped in front of her. There was a coil of rope on the floor, which she had fallen over. Sitting back, she ran her fingers gingerly across the top of her head, near the hairline. She felt a small swelling, and her head throbbed painfully.

Nancy tried to envision the different kinds of camping gear she had seen on the shelves when her flashlight was working. She couldn't think of a thing that would pick a lock.

Discouraged, her head throbbing, she felt the bump on her head for the second time, and her hand brushed against a barrette. A barrette! Nancy thought with relief. It was old, with two thin, flexible prongs. Nancy had a way out.

With the barrette in her hand, Nancy stood up and walked back to the door. A moment later the door swung open and Nancy stepped into the main office. As she closed the gear room door behind her, a bright flashlight shone directly into her eyes, blinding her. Nancy froze.

"Nancy, what happened?" Ned calmly questioned.

"Oh, I'm so glad it's you," Nancy cried, rushing toward him.

"Who else would it be?" Ned asked, confused.

"I don't know," Nancy admitted. "But someone locked me in the gear room and then I fell and hit my head."

"I don't like the sound of that, Nan," Ned said.

Before long Nancy and Ned were in the car again, driving back to the hotel.

"When you hadn't come back in twenty-five minutes, I was sure something had gone wrong, so I went in after you," Ned was saying. "I'm just sorry I didn't go in sooner."

"You did the right thing, Ned." Nancy reached over and squeezed his arm. "But are you sure you didn't see anyone going into or coming out of the office?"

"I'm positive," Ned responded. "I had my eyes on the front door the whole time you were inside, and nobody went through it."

"They must have come in through a side

door," Nancy concluded. "Unless they were already inside. I just wish we knew who it was."

When Nancy's wake-up call came at six o'clock the next morning, it was still dark outside. She had to be at Alpine Adventures at seven-thirty and still had last-minute packing to do. After taking a shower, she rolled her sleeping bag up and stuffed it into the bottom of the backpack that Alpine Adventures had supplied. Then she laid out all the clothing she'd need.

By the time Nancy had squeezed everything into her pack, strapped her thermal sleeping pad to the outside, and dressed, it was time to meet Ned for the drive over to Alpine Adventures.

"Bring your packs over here," Logan called as Nancy and Ned pulled them out of the trunk of their car.

"I don't know how we're going to carry these packs up a fourteen-thousand-foot mountain," Ned murmured as they made their way to the van.

"We only have to carry them to base camp," Nancy offered as reassurance.

"That's a two-day hike," Ned countered anxiously. "And even *it's* at ten thousand feet."

101

Nancy smiled confidently. "I know you can handle it," she said.

Nancy and Ned next went into the office to put on their boots and crampons so that Kara could check their fit.

With everything loaded, the group piled into the van and set off for the park. Kara had brought along warm muffins, fruit, tea, and coffee, and everyone ate as the van made its way along country highways, with Mt. Rainier beckoning in the distance.

Nancy squeezed Ned's hand as she gazed at the tall evergreens, their branches laden with white, powdery snow. The early-morning sky was clear and brilliant.

After a two-and-a-half-hour drive they climbed out of the van, and everyone gasped at Rainier. Almost completely covered in snow, it dwarfed the other mountains. They were at fifty-five hundred feet, and the remaining nine thousand feet —straight up—looked impossible to climb.

Hefting their packs and strapping snowshoes onto their boots, the group hiked over several flat, open spaces before beginning the ascent to Panorama Point.

As they hiked along, the conversation turned

from the weather to climbing experiences and gruesome climbing accidents. Hundreds of people had died on the mountain, many of them on the lower slopes and lesser peaks.

"Hikers don't realize that there's danger at lower altitudes, too," Kara explained. "They think they're on safe, gentle territory, so they don't pay attention to what they're doing or where they're hiking, which is when accidents happen."

Nancy felt a sense of foreboding as she lifted her snowshoes, keeping in rhythm with the other hikers. The mountain was unquestionably a dangerous one, with its glaciers, snow bridges, and crevasses, and it was even more dangerous with a possible criminal on the trip.

Sometime in midafternoon, the group arrived at their first camp near Panorama Point.

"This is it," Alex declared, gesturing widely with his arms.

Nancy wondered exactly what he meant. The area was generally flat, with a sloping hill on one side that provided some shelter from the wind. A clump of fir trees stood off to the right, and there were a few rocky ledges about fifty yards away. They were in the middle of nowhere.

"We're going to build snow caves," Kara explained when she saw the confusion on Nancy's face. "They're the warmest shelter out here."

Nancy nodded and took her pack off, setting it on the snow near everyone else's. She marveled at the weightlessness she felt as she walked over to the group that had gathered near the hill.

"Okay," Logan began as he unstrapped a small collapsible shovel from his backpack. "Alex and I are each going to start a cave by digging two holes into the side of this hill." While Nancy and the rest of the group watched, the two men dug narrow tubelike holes into the side of the hill, about twenty-five feet apart.

"The holes should be just wide enough for one person to fit through," Alex explained as he worked at the icy snow with his shovel. The two men dug for several minutes. While they worked, the others cleared the snow away from the openings, though Eladio was worried about getting snow in his boots.

Alex and Logan then wriggled themselves into the holes and each began to create a room. They shoved snow out through the holes, and the teams on the outside cleared it away.

Eventually the caves were large enough for a second person to fit inside, so Nancy crawled inside one and began to help clear the space. It didn't take long for Nancy to realize that building a snow cave was difficult, tedious work. Because the entrances to the cave were long and narrow, she had to shovel the snow out in very small amounts.

The group worked on the caves for almost two hours, and when they were finished they had built two caves that each measured seven feet by seven feet—big enough for four people each.

As she set up her plastic liner and sleeping bag, Nancy commented how warm it was in the cave.

"This must be your first time in a snow cave," Lisa said knowingly.

Nancy was slightly irritated by her tone, but she smiled graciously. "Is it that obvious?" she asked.

"Not really," Anne assured her as she spread her thermal sleeping pad on the ground. Nancy was surprised that Anne had come to her defense. "But unless you've done a lot of winter climbing or spent time in the Arctic, there's no reason why you *would* spend time in a snow cave."

"I guess that's true," Nancy agreed, laughing. "I'd really miss having electricity." Having placed her sleeping bag on top of her thermal pad, Nancy decided to rejoin the rest of the group.

Wriggling out of the cave entrance, Nancy shivered and pulled her scarf up around her face. It was much colder outside.

Kara and Logan had set up a kind of shelter with tarps and were cooking dinner. Nancy walked over to the "kitchen" and poured boiling water into her bowl to heat it up. Logan had explained that if you put hot food into a frozen bowl, the food didn't stay warm for long.

"Lots of carbohydrates," Kara joked as she filled Nancy and Ned's bowls with macaroni and cheese.

Ned and Nancy turned to go back into Ned's snow cave to eat. They huddled close together on Ned's sleeping bag, trying to keep warm as they ate.

When dinner was finished, Nancy and Ned went back outside. They asked Kara if she needed help with cleanup, but she insisted that everything was under control. Kara shooed everyone away from the kitchen area and began to do the dishes, so Nancy decided to turn in.

"Sleep tight," Ned said to Nancy as he wrapped his arms around her shoulders and gave her a tender kiss. His mouth was warm compared to the cold mountain air, and Nancy felt herself melting in his arms.

"I will," Nancy promised, feeling how tired she was. After giving Ned a final kiss good night, she crawled into her cave.

Since she had been the first to turn in, the snow cave was empty. Nancy pulled off her gloves, parka, and wind pants, leaving her hat and wool socks on for warmth.

After burrowing into her mummy-shaped sleeping bag, Nancy considered what the next day might bring.

A moment later her thoughts were interrupted by a loud scream that echoed through the night.

Chapter

Twelve

Nancy sat bolt upright. It was Kara who had screamed. In an instant Nancy was out of her sleeping bag and pulling on her boots and parka.

Nancy squirmed outside and saw Alex pulling Kara up over an icy ledge about forty yards from the camping area.

"What happened?" Nancy asked Ned as they watched Alex lift Kara to safety.

"I don't know," he answered. "I was just getting settled into my sleeping bag when I heard her scream. I got out here just before you did."

"She's okay," Alex told Nancy and the rest of

the group, who had come to see what was going on. "You can go back to what you were doing."

"What happened?" Nancy asked when she reached Alex and Kara.

"Someone pushed me," Kara responded, her voice shaking. "I was standing outside, relaxing, before settling in for the night. When I walked by the ledge, I felt someone shove me over the edge."

"Are you hurt?" Nancy asked.

"No, I'm fine," Kara answered, but it was obvious she was shaken up.

"Could you tell if it was a man or a woman?" Nancy asked, lowering her voice.

"No," Kara said helplessly. "It happened too fast. I was right by the edge, so it wouldn't have taken much strength to push me over."

Nancy walked over to the area and shined her flashlight on the icy snow. She was hoping to find footprints, but the snow was so hard there were very few indentations. There was nothing discernible.

"Somebody wants you out of the way, and they're taking bold steps to make it happen," Nancy said. Maybe it hadn't been such a good idea to let Lisa come on the trip, she thought.

They couldn't possibly keep an eye on her at every moment. And what about Anne?

"We've got to remember to keep a close eye on Lisa and Anne. I'm sure no one will try to pull another stunt like this." *I hope* not, anyway, she thought to herself.

Having done all the investigating she could do in the dark, Nancy went back to her snow cave and snuggled into her sleeping bag. As she tried to fall asleep, she couldn't help but wonder what else would happen before the end of the trip.

The next morning the group ate a breakfast of hot oatmeal before repacking all their gear and continuing up the mountain. It was another perfect day for climbing, about ten degrees with a clear sky and not too much wind. The slope was steeper as they made their way onto the Paradise Glaciers. Kara led the group, with Logan in the middle and Alex at the rear. He made sure Lisa was directly in front of him and as far from Kara as possible. Alex and Logan had also done a thorough gear check that morning to make sure that nothing had been sabotaged.

"You should all be pressure-breathing," Logan called to the group from behind Nancy. A moment later she heard him exhaling noisily, *"Phhhhshhhhh."*

Nancy began to do the breathing exercise, even though she wasn't feeling the effects of the altitude. She felt silly making so much noise, but after a few minutes the noisy exhalation seemed natural.

Nancy began to think about the case, trying to piece together what she knew. Lisa Osterman was still her best suspect, though she wasn't sure what the girl's motive could be. Lisa could have pushed Kara over the edge. But so could almost anyone, Nancy knew—including Anne Bolle.

How did Hank Moody fit in with all this? That ticket payment tied him to Lisa—and to the case as well. Nancy sighed heavily and looked up at the beautiful sky. It was dotted with puffy clouds that were so close she could almost touch them.

After an hour and a half of climbing, the group stopped on a ledge for a break. Nancy had grown quite warm during the rugged climb and had loosened her scarf. But after standing still for just a few minutes, Nancy felt herself getting chilled. She pulled her scarf tightly around her neck and pulled her hat snugly down around her ears.

"Are you chilly?" Ned asked, coming up behind her and rubbing her shoulders vigorously.

Nancy nodded as Kara spoke up. "Be sure you're bundled up well," she said to the group. "When you're standing still, your body doesn't produce that extra heat, and it doesn't take long for the chilly temperature to get to you."

"Also, I want to see all of you drinking from your water bottles," Logan told everyone. "You may not think you're thirsty, but you're losing water as you sweat, so drink up."

Nancy pulled her water bottle out from inside her parka, where it was carried to keep the water from freezing. After taking a sip, she handed the bottle to Ned.

"Thanks," he murmured.

Kara opened a bag of nuts, raisins, and sunflower seeds and passed them around. Nancy wasn't feeling hungry, but dutifully took a handful.

She passed the bag to Eladio, who paused for a second. "Could you scoop me up a handful and put it into my glove?" he finally asked her.

Nancy laughed, reached inside to pull out a handful, and carefully let the contents fall into Eladio's gloved palm.

After everyone had a chance to eat, drink, and take a short rest, the group began climbing again. Moving slowly, they made their way up the Paradise Glaciers—snow-covered masses of ice with occasional rocks jutting out on either side.

At one point the group had to cross a five-foot snow bridge, which Nancy learned was several thin layers of snow covering a deep crevasse. A snow bridge was sometimes the only way to cross a hundred-foot-deep crevasse, though most crevasses were narrow enough to step across. Some snow bridges were several feet thick, while others were just a few inches, in which case they would collapse under a person's weight.

"Just walk slowly and surely, and stay in the center," Logan advised Nancy from behind. "You'll do fine."

Nancy's heart raced as she stepped onto the bridge, which was about five feet across. She was tempted to run across it as fast as she could, but knew that was the worst thing she could do.

After about five heart-wrenching steps, Nancy reached the other side and solid ground. Heaving a sigh of relief, she continued up the icy glacier after the others.

When the group was just below Anvil Rock, they stopped for lunch, settling into a snowbank that protected them from the wind. They were at nine thousand five hundred feet.

"Are you all right?" Nancy asked Eladio, who was quite pale.

"I'm fine," he said. "I'm just not hungry."

"After all that climbing, I'm starved," Ned put in, reaching for a sandwich.

Nancy looked at the lunch of cheese and salami on whole-grain bread. With a pang she realized that she didn't feel hungry either. The altitude was starting to get to her. "I'm not hungry," she admitted to Eladio. "But if we eat, I'm sure we'll feel better."

"Everyone has to eat at least half a sandwich." Kara coached. "If you don't keep fueling yourselves, your bodies will shut down and we won't make it to the top."

Nancy reached for a sandwich, and by the fourth bite found it actually tasted good.

As everyone ate, the conversation drifted to Camp Muir, where they'd be staying that night.

"It marks the line between the upper and the lower mountains," Alex explained. "Most people who climb the mountain from the south use it as a takeoff point for the summit."

"How many people go through Camp Muir in the winter?" Eladio asked.

"Not too many," Kara answered. "Maybe a

hundred. Though over a thousand might come through in a single summer season," she added.

"Does anybody want another sandwich?" Alex asked, holding up what was left of the salami. When nobody responded, he put the bread and meat back into his backpack.

When they started off again, Nancy listened to the sound of everyone pressure-breathing.

Within an hour and a half they reached Camp Muir. Perched on one side of a ridge, Camp Muir consisted of five buildings, most of which were mainly buried under snow. The group would stay in the largest building, which was reserved for public use.

It was getting dark, but nevertheless the view from the camp was incredible.

"That's Cadaver Gap," Logan said, pointing to the space between Cathedral Rocks and Gibraltar Rock. "But it's not half as scary as it sounds," he assured the group.

In spite of the fact that the stone building wasn't heated and was very cold, everyone was relieved to get inside, out of the wind. The building was sparsely furnished—two tiers of bunks were situated on the far side of the room. Since there wasn't a table or chairs, Alex suggested they put their thermal sleeping pads and sleeping bags on the floor to sit on.

Logan and Kara began to cook another meal.

"I'm beginning to think that eating is the only thing we do," Eladio murmured.

"We'll be climbing again before we know it," Anne offered. "So it's really important to keep food in our stomachs."

Eladio checked his watch, which read five o'clock. "Twelve hours," he said, "and we'll be heading for the top." Alex had explained that they'd start the climb at five A.M., so they could make it to the summit and back before nightfall. "Will we be crossing many more snow bridges?" Eladio asked Anne.

"I'm not sure," she admitted.

Nancy shivered, remembering the experience of crossing the bridge. "That was scary. I wanted to run across as fast as I could."

"That's the hardest part," Lisa agreed, joining in the conversation.

Eladio pulled out a deck of playing cards, and the group began playing gin rummy. It was difficult to hold the cards with gloves, but it was too cold to take them off. While they played, Nancy observed Anne, whose attention was on Logan. It seemed as if Anne wanted more than friendship from him, Nancy thought. Maybe that's why she'd lied about her whereabouts on the night of the break-in.

Later, as they sat around eating chicken stew, they talked some more about that day's hike and what the next one might be like. Without warning the front door burst open, and Nancy gasped when she saw the person framed in the doorway. It was Hank Moody!

Chapter

Thirteen

WHILE NANCY STARED in surprise, Hank stepped into the room with another man right behind him. She remembered her suspicions about Lisa and Hank, and turned to Lisa. The expression on the young woman's face was unmistakable—she was scared.

Without greeting the group, Hank walked up to Alex and spoke to him in a low voice, leaving the other man near the door.

Nancy watched the two men, and after a few moments Alex spoke. "That would be fine, Hank," he said congenially. "There's plenty of room." He gestured to a row of empty bunks at the back of the shelter.

Hank nodded gruffly and turned to the man with whom he had come in. "Let's bring our gear inside," he said, and the two men left. A few moments later they returned with two large packs and ice axes.

Although Nancy wasn't hungry, she went up for a second helping of food so she could hear what Logan and Alex were saying. Logan was telling Alex that he thought it was a mistake to share the shelter with Hank.

"He's up to no good," Logan was saying. "Why else would he show up here?"

"He's already on the mountain, so we may as well make the best of the situation," Alex reasoned. "If he stays with us, we'll at least be able to watch him."

Shaking his head, Logan poured himself a cup of tea and leaned against the single bench that ran along the wall.

Carrying another bowl of chicken stew, Nancy rejoined her group. While she ate, she watched for signals between Lisa and Hank, but they didn't even glance at each other.

Everyone drank a cup of tea and ate some

cookies for dessert. Eladio and Ned started up another game of cards, but Nancy was too worked up to play. Standing up to stretch, Nancy scanned the room and noticed that both Lisa and Hank were missing.

"Have you seen Lisa?" she asked Alex.

"No," he admitted cautiously. "I haven't. She must be outside."

"I've got a feeling she's with Hank," Nancy said grimly. "I'm going to see if I can find them."

"Be careful," Kara advised. "And take your flashlight. It's really dark."

Nancy dug her flashlight out of her pack and pulled on thick gloves and a hat, then zipped up her jacket. When she opened the door, a gust of cold wind chilled her. She adjusted her scarf and turned on her flashlight as she stepped into the night.

Nancy cast the flashlight's faint glow over the white snow and moved carefully along the rock saddle. Their shelter stood on one end of the ridge, opposite the other buildings. Nancy guessed that Hank and Lisa would meet in one of those buildings, as far as possible from the rest of the group.

Even with her flashlight, Nancy found the

going difficult because the ground was so uneven. Though it was mostly clear, clouds covered the moon from time to time, leaving just the flashlight to pierce the expansive darkness.

Nancy walked slowly, shining her light just slightly in front her. She was fairly confident that the wind would drown out the noise of her footsteps, but she tried to step quietly, just in case.

When she was about fifty yards from the first building on the other side of the ridge, the ground flattened and the walking became easier. Turning off her flashlight, Nancy stood in the darkness for a moment, listening. The wind howled and echoed off the giant mountain, but Nancy didn't hear any human voices.

Nancy began making her way toward the snow-covered buildings again, using the light of the moon to guide her. She made her way between the small kitchen hut and the larger building that served as a sleeping quarters. She walked around both buildings twice, but nobody was there.

They could be anywhere, Nancy realized, suddenly feeling that her search was hopeless. Disappointed, she turned her flashlight on again and walked back toward her shelter. The wind was blowing in her face now, and she shivered in the darkness. When she finally reached the shelter, she felt a sense of relief.

As Nancy started to pull the door open, she heard voices from the side of the building. Lisa and Hank! Quickly Nancy moved into the shadows, straining to hear what they were saying.

"I told you I'd take care of it," said Lisa, her voice a high-pitched whisper.

"Are you sure you've got it under control?" Hank asked. "You know that everything's riding on this."

"I'm a grown woman with mountaineering experience," Lisa responded. "You know that, Uncle Hank. That's why you asked me to do this, remember?"

Uncle Hank? So that was it, Nancy mused. Lisa Osterman must be Hank Moody's niece! *She* was the child in the photo in Hank's office who looked so familiar. She was obviously trying to help her uncle beat the competition.

"I don't know if this was such a good—"

"I can handle it," Lisa said anxiously. "Now please just go back down the mountain before you cause trouble. Logan Miller is already suspicious of you, and your being here will only make things worse, especially for me."

"The guide I brought with me wants to climb the mountain tomorrow," Hank said. "And I promised him we could. But we'll start up ahead of your group so we'll be a good distance from you."

There was silence for a few moments, then Lisa spoke again. "I don't like it," she said. "But I can't stop you."

A second later Nancy heard footsteps coming toward her. Having no time to get out of Lisa's way, she quickly ducked deeper into the shadows. Lisa stomped past her in a matter of moments, not realizing that Nancy was there. When she had gone inside, Nancy moved away from the building. She didn't want to draw attention to herself by going inside right after Lisa, so she waited for a few minutes in the darkness before entering.

Nancy was eager to tell Kara and Alex her news, but they had both turned in. Eladio and Anne were still playing rummy, but Ned had gone to sleep, too. Nancy checked her watch and realized that it was almost ten o'clock. In seven hours they'd start their climb to the top of the mountain, and she knew she'd better get some rest. Nancy took off her hat, gloves, and parka and climbed into her sleeping bag. Minutes later she was fast asleep.

"Wake up, sleepyhead," Ned said as he bent over to give Nancy a light kiss on her cold nose. Nancy opened her eyes and saw Ned smiling down at her. "It's time to get something to eat," he told her. "We'll be leaving soon."

Remembering the conversation she'd overheard between Hank and Lisa, Nancy wriggled out of her sleeping bag and found Alex and Kara to tell them the news.

"Hank has already headed up the mountain," Kara said. "They were gone when I woke up about forty minutes ago."

"He said he'd start before we did and stay away from our group," Nancy told them.

"We'll just have to keep doing what we've been doing," Alex concluded. "Keep a close eye on Lisa and double-check all the equipment."

"Right," Nancy agreed.

After a breakfast of hot oatmeal with nuts and raisins, the group filed outside in the darkness.

"We rope together at this point because the glaciers are more treacherous above ten thousand feet," Alex explained, holding up a rope. "The first stretch this morning is easy, but we'll rope together now into two groups so we don't have to do it on an incline."

Once everyone was secured by a rope, Kara started off as leader of the first group again, with Lisa bringing up the rear. Alex was right behind her as leader of the second group. Ned was right behind Kara, and Nancy behind him.

The nearly full moon hung over the edge of Gibraltar Rock and lit up the darkness when it wasn't covered by clouds. Far up ahead, the shadowy figures of Hank and his climbing partner could be seen, making their way up the mountain.

When the forty feet of rope between Ned and Nancy was taut, Nancy began to move. Her crampons crunched beneath her as she walked through the silent winter air.

The first stretch was fairly easy, but soon the group climbed up a steep slope with icy debris that made the going slow. Finally they were at the top of Cathedral Rocks, and from there it was on to the Ingraham Glacier.

It was still dark, and the moon was now completely covered with clouds. As the group sat down to rest, it began to snow.

"This is eerie," Eladio said as they munched nuts in the darkness.

"I feel like we're on the moon or something," said Ned. "There's nobody around for miles and miles."

"Except Hank and his partner," Nancy put in.

When everyone had eaten something, the group started walking again, making its way up the Ingraham Glacier. This stretch was considerably steeper, and Nancy had to concentrate on pressure-breathing to keep an altitude headache at bay.

After the group had walked another forty-five minutes, the sun began to rise. Nancy could see that they were on a section of glacier laced with crevasses. She followed Ned, stepping across the narrow crevasses while trying not to think about the hundred-foot ice-lined cracks she was walking over.

As she stepped over a third crevasse, Nancy heard a rumbling echo. The rumbling grew louder, and Nancy knew what it was—an avalanche. It sounded as though it was heading straight toward them!

Chapter

Fourteen

"AVALANCHE!" KARA SHOUTED from above. "Arrest!"

Nancy plunged her ice ax into the icy slope and did a spread eagle, digging her crampons into the ice. She closed her eyes and a moment later her ears rang with the rumble of falling ice and snow. Her heart thudded in her chest as she waited for the impact. Surprisingly, none came. When she opened her eyes a few minutes later, she saw masses of ice and snow moving down the mountain about two hundred yards to her left. Realizing they were safe, Nancy breathed a sigh of relief.

When the echo of falling debris had died away, Kara told the climbers in her group to pull out of their arrests. They climbed to a safe resting spot and waited for Alex's group to catch up. As Nancy sat down, she realized that it was snowing harder and the wind had picked up.

"M-m-my uncle," Lisa blurted out in a state of panic. "He's farther up the mountain. He could be trapped!" As soon as the words were out of her mouth Lisa stopped, realizing that she'd blown her cover.

"Your uncle?" Nancy asked, acting as if she knew nothing about this.

Lisa cast her eyes down, not wanting to gaze at Nancy. "Hank Moody is my uncle," she admitted.

"So why aren't you climbing with him?" Nancy asked evenly. Lisa's head shot up as if she were going to defend herself, and her eyes met Nancy's blue stare. "I think you've got some explaining to do," Nancy finished.

Lisa looked at Kara and Ned, and then back at Nancy. She sighed. "My uncle wanted to find out why Alpine Adventures does such good business," she began. "I didn't want to have anything to do with this at first," she pleaded. "But he was losing business every day and getting more and more desperate, so I finally agreed. It seemed perfectly harmless," Lisa went on, "until I found Nancy snooping around my uncle's office."

"So that was *you*," Nancy said, remembering her experience in Hank Moody's gear room.

Lisa's eyes grew wide. "I'm really sorry," she said earnestly. "I was afraid you'd find out who I was, and I panicked. I ran off and locked you in the storage room. I didn't mean to scare you," she finished. "Really, I didn't."

"Did you break into Alpine Adventures, too?" Kara asked pointedly.

Lisa's eyes widened. "No," she said. "I didn't even know about the break-in until I overheard Logan talking about it." Her eyes darted from Kara to Nancy. "I didn't do anything else," she said solemnly. "Honest."

"And your uncle?" Nancy asked. "What about him?"

"As far as I know, he's only guilty of spying," she said.

"But *you* lied about your climbing experience." Kara was not about to let Lisa off the hook easily.

"Sort of," Lisa admitted. "I've done a lot of climbing, but only in North America. I've never climbed in the Himalayas."

"I thought so." Kara stared coldly at Lisa for a moment, then something inside her softened. "But I suppose no real harm was done," she said. "In spite of everything, we'll do what we can to help your uncle," she said.

"Oh, thank you," Lisa cried, wiping frozen tears from her cheeks.

After hearing Lisa's story, Nancy felt a sense of foreboding. She believed what Lisa had told them, which meant that the villain was still out there. And Nancy had no clue who it was.

Within a few minutes the second group had arrived at the resting point.

"That avalanche was awfully close," Alex said, pausing to gaze up at the sky. "And I think there's a storm setting in. I don't think we should be climbing in these conditions."

"You mean we have to go back?" Eladio asked incredulously.

"I'm afraid so," Alex answered. "There's no reason to take unnecessary risks. With so few people climbing in the winter, there's no ranger stationed at Camp Muir. And they aren't well set up for rescues. It's best if we head down tonight and hope for a change in the weather. If it improves, we can try again tomorrow. We have plenty of supplies, and we'll be safe at Camp Muir."

"But my uncle," Lisa wailed. "He's up on the mountain!"

Alex looked at Lisa blankly for a moment, and then Kara and Nancy recounted Lisa's story. "She's afraid that he's trapped farther up the mountain," Kara finished.

"It's possible." Alex's expression grew dark. He was quiet for a moment, and then he turned to Logan. "I think you and I will have to keep climbing to see what's happened," Alex said.

"I'm not sure that's the best solution," Logan answered. "I mean, I'm willing to go, but I think that Kara might be the best person to go with me. She's an expert in rescue techniques."

"He's right," Kara agreed. "I should go in your place, Alex."

"Maybe we should go together," Alex suggested.

"I don't mean to sound morbid," Anne offered, "but if anything were to happen to both of you, Allie would—"

"You're right, of course," Alex said, cutting Anne off before the awful words were out of her mouth. His face was tight with anguish. Stepping

131

forward, he gave his wife a hug and a kiss. "Be careful," he said.

"I will," she whispered, holding him close for a few extra seconds.

The decision made, Logan and Kara roped together and began climbing farther up the mountain. The rest of the group tied into a second rope and started on the hour-long descent to Camp Muir.

With Alex in front and Anne in the rear, the group moved as quickly as it could down Ingraham Glacier. The snow was falling heavily now, and it was difficult to see where the crevasses were. Nancy nearly slipped and fell several times.

On top of Cathedral Rocks Alex made everyone stop to eat something, even though they were all eager to get to the safety and shelter of Camp Muir.

Nancy felt a sense of relief when her feet touched the flatter, more secure ground of Cowlitz Glacier. Unfortunately, the flat openness made it the perfect place for howling winds and falling snow to gather speed. Nancy squinted through the snow as she made her way across this final stretch to camp.

Within another half hour the group had arrived safely back at Camp Muir. Alex immediately used the radio in the shelter to call the ranger, but just as he had feared, they were shorthanded and couldn't send a chopper up unless there was a definite emergency.

"But there may be two people trapped by an avalanche on the upper Ingraham Glacier," Alex said into the radio's receiver.

"I realize that," the ranger's voice crackled over the radio. "But you're talking about a rescue at twelve thousand feet. I can't bring the helicopter to that kind of elevation unless I'm certain it's absolutely necessary, especially with the storm that's setting in. I know you feel helpless, and I do, too. But I can't do it."

"No," Alex responded, sighing. "I suppose you can't."

"Let me know if anything further develops," the ranger said.

"I will," Alex said. Then he signed off.

Meanwhile, the rest of the group was sitting in a group on the floor, trying to comfort Lisa. "Your uncle will be fine," Eladio was saying. "He's been climbing for more than twenty years."

"But if he was hit by an avalanche, his experience wouldn't matter," Lisa said through her tears. "Avalanches kill hundreds of people every year."

Nancy knew that what Lisa said was true, and in spite of all the lies the young woman had told in the past few days, Nancy's heart went out to her.

"Kara is one of the best mountaineers in the country," Anne said as she put an arm around Lisa. "If anyone can handle this situation, she can."

Lisa smiled weakly. "I know," she said, wiping her eyes. "It's just that I feel so helpless."

"We all do," Anne said quietly. "We just have to think positively while we wait it out."

"And know that the two best people for the job are out there trying to find your uncle right now," Ned added. "Because Logan knows exactly what he's doing, too."

"I bet Alex will be sorry to lose Logan," Nancy commented.

"Where's he going?" Anne asked.

"He's been offered a sponsorship by Recreational Gear," Nancy explained. "He'll be going on the European tour in about a month."

Confusion crossed Anne's face as she listened to Nancy. "That's impossible," she said, shaking her head. "They've just offered *me* a sponsorship, and they only take one climber a year."

"Are you sure?" Nancy asked, thinking that information might be important to the case. "Maybe the company has made an exception."

"No," Anne said matter-of-factly. "I just spoke with them this week, and they said that I'll be their only climber this year." She leaned toward Nancy. "And believe me," she said in a whisper, "I'd love it if Logan and I were sponsored by the same company." She smiled knowingly, and Nancy knew for sure that Anne was hoping for a relationship with Logan. But she didn't have time to think about that. . . .

Images of Logan over the past few days were flashing through Nancy's mind. Logan had tried to suggest that Alex's car accident was the result of bald tires, when in fact the vehicle had been sabotaged. He had also said that he was a car buff—that he liked to tinker around with engines. That meant that he probably had the know-how to mess up the steering on Kara's car.

Nancy next remembered overhearing Logan try to convince Tsu to let him go on the trip in her place. The very next day Tsu was injured so that she *couldn't* go on the climb. As an active climber, Logan could have fixed the rope so that it would break without making it too obvious.

Logan had also given Alex an ultimatum when it looked as if he was going to be passed over for taking Tsu's place on the Rainier trip. The ultimatum had seemed normal at the time, but now Nancy guessed that it was all part of his plan. Logan must have known that his friend would give in.

Why would Logan have lied about his sponsorship at Recreational Gear, though? Nancy wondered. Probably to divert suspicion from himself, she concluded. Then everyone would think he had a great future and no reason to resent Kara for edging him out of Alpine Adventures.

With a sense of dread, Nancy recalled Logan suggesting that Kara would be the best person to go up the mountain with him.

A shiver ran up Nancy's spine as she realized that Logan could well be the villain. And he was out on the mountain with Kara right now—in the middle of a snowstorm!

Chapter

Fifteen

HORRIFIED, NANCY PULLED Alex aside. "Alex," she whispered. "I've got some awful news."

"With four people on the mountain in a storm and no chance for a rescue, I don't think things could get much worse," Alex responded dryly. "What is it?" he finally asked.

"I think Logan has been causing all the trouble," Nancy said.

"That's impossible, Nancy. Logan is my best friend. He'd never do anything to hurt me or Alpine Adventures."

"He gave up a lot to come and set up this

business with you, and now that Kara's getting back into climbing—"

"But that doesn't matter anymore," Alex interrupted. "He's got a terrific sponsorship, and his climbing future has never been brighter."

"His sponsorship is a lie—it doesn't exist," Nancy said.

"How do you know?" Alex questioned.

"Anne just told me the company is sponsoring her—and she's their only climber this year."

"And you believe Anne—Kara's competitor —over Logan?" Alex asked incredulously.

He had a point, and Nancy realized that Alex would have a hard time thinking Logan was anything but a good friend. She felt certain, though, that her suspicions were correct—she just had to make him see it. So she rattled off the clues that had brought her to her conclusion.

"Look, Nancy," Alex said angrily when she'd finished. "Logan and I have been through everything together. I don't expect you to understand this, but he'd do anything for me. And I'd do anything for him."

"Would you let him kill your wife?" Nancy asked quietly.

"Of course not," Alex responded hotly. "But he *wouldn't* hurt her. That's what I'm telling you.

I trust Logan completely. In fact, he's the only person who knows about your investigation besides Kara and me."

"What?" Nancy's eyes widened.

"It seemed silly to keep it from him," Alex said, uncomfortably. "I tell Logan everything."

"When exactly did you tell him?" Nancy questioned.

"On Friday morning. He said he didn't think the police were going to follow through on things, and it seemed natural to tell him that you were working on the case, so I did," he answered.

"He never let on to me that he knew," Nancy said. "Why do you suppose he'd keep that from me?"

"I don't know," Alex admitted. "Come to think of it, that's when he told me that he thought Hank Moody was responsible. I thought it was a little odd that he said it just at that point, because we'd been talking about the case for at least fifteen minutes and he hadn't mentioned that he thought it was Hank until then."

Nancy was finally getting through to Alex.

Just then Ned approached the two of them. "Nancy," he said excitedly, "Anne just told me something that I think might be important. The annual guide presentation was canceled this year," he said. "Apparently not enough people signed up, so they called it off a few days before the event."

"Logan's alibi is gone," Nancy said, nodding. "He told me he was at the presentation the night of the break-in."

Just then, Anne approached them somewhat sheepishly. "I've a confession to make," she told them. "I didn't have dinner with friends in Seattle last Wednesday. I had dinner in Enumclaw with Logan. He made me promise to keep our date a secret. I thought maybe he had another girlfriend, but now I realize he didn't want me to wreck his alibi."

"You're right, Nancy," Alex said. "I hate to admit it, but it must be Logan. I've got to go after them."

"I'm coming with you," Nancy said.

"No." Alex shook his head. "It's too dangerous."

"Alex, you can't go out there alone," Nancy said with determination.

He paused for a moment, then nodded slowly. "All right."

Within minutes, Nancy and Alex were roped together and ready to go.

Ned gave Nancy a kiss goodbye. "Take care,"

he whispered as he gave her a last-minute squeeze.

Nancy nodded. "I will," she said. Then she and Alex headed back up the mountain.

The snow was tapering off and the clouds seemed to be dispersing, but the wind was fierce. Nancy was instantly chilled.

With the wind whipping around her, Nancy began to question the wisdom of their search. The snow had completely covered any tracks that might have been left behind. With a sinking feeling, Nancy realized that it was possible they would miss Logan and Kara altogether.

Nancy didn't hear Alex shout a warning until it was too late. As she stepped forward, Nancy slipped and fell, on the edge of a crevasse. Her legs dangled over the edge of the deep ice crack. Instinctively, Nancy dug her ice ax into the glacier to keep herself from slipping any farther while Alex came to help her. He pulled her up and away from the crevasse.

Sitting near the edge of the glacier, Nancy realized how exhausted she was. There wasn't time to be tired; she had to keep going, she knew.

Nancy finally stood up. "Let's go," she said.

The two continued up the glacier, passing the point where they had turned back earlier. By now the snow had stopped completely. The clouds were dispersing, and at moments the sunlight was painfully bright.

"We've been making good time," Alex called back.

Nancy nodded and kept moving forward. Her legs and head were throbbing, but she steeled herself as she continued to put one foot in front of the other.

"Look!" Alex shouted minutes later. "It's them!"

Nancy recognized Logan and Kara about two hundred yards ahead, standing still. She and Alex began walking faster. When they were about thirty yards away, Nancy realized that Logan and Kara weren't just standing—they were struggling with each other, right at the edge of a wide crevasse!

"I gave up my career for this company, and I won't be shut out now," Logan was shouting.

"Logan, no," Alex shouted, closing in on him.

Just then Logan pulled something out of his pocket—and with a gasp Nancy saw that he had a knife.

He grabbed the rope that held him and Kara together and sliced through it in a single, quick motion. Then he pushed Kara toward the edge of the crevasse!

At that same moment Alex cut himself free from Nancy and hurled himself toward Logan. Kara fell into the crevasse, her rope trailing behind her.

While Alex and Logan struggled, Nancy loosened her rope and crawled to the edge of the crevasse. Looking down, she was horrified by what she saw. The crevasse was about two hundred feet deep, and Kara was clinging to the side of it about a quarter of the way down!

Chapter

Sixteen

Nancy realized that it was up to her to rescue Kara.

"I'm going to rig a pulley system to get you out," Nancy called down to Kara.

"Please hurry," Kara called up. "I don't know how long I can hold on."

Nancy grabbed her picket anchor and began to pound it into the ice about six feet from the edge of the crevasse.

When the anchor was about halfway in, Nancy saw Logan move toward her. He had his ice ax raised, ready to strike. Without stopping to think, Nancy gave Logan a high karate kick, which sent him flying across the ice. He hit his head and was out.

Alex got up and came to help Nancy pound in the anchor. They rigged a pulley system, tying the rope around Nancy, and then Alex lowered her into the crevasse. Keeping her arms and legs directly in front of herself, Nancy moved slowly down the ice face into the crevasse.

In a few minutes Nancy had reached Kara and tied her into her rope.

"Oh, Nancy." Kara shuddered. "I'm so glad to see you."

Nancy and Kara then began the climb back up the crevasse wall. Alex pulled from above.

As the two women reached the top of the crevasse, the thrum of a helicopter's rotors echoed off the mountain as the copter landed. Ned climbed out first, followed by a ranger and a police officer.

"I'm Nancy Drew," Nancy said. "I'm a private investigator, and that man should be arrested for attempted murder." She pointed to Logan, who was just coming to.

"He pushed this woman into that two-hundred-foot crevasse," she added.

The officer approached Logan, who willingly held his wrists up for the cuffs.

"Ned," Nancy asked, "how did you get the ranger to send a helicopter? And how did you know where we'd be?"

"I told them I was a private investigator and that my partner needed backup for a mountain emergency." He grinned. "The ranger guessed this is where he'd strike."

They all managed to fit in the chopper.

"That was a brave thing you did, miss," the officer yelled to Nancy over the noise. "Following a criminal up the mountain like that."

"I had someone along to help," Nancy said, nodding at Alex.

Logan was sitting in the corner next to the police officer. His face was stained with tears.

"I didn't mean it," he said hoarsely. "I didn't mean it. But I couldn't watch her get back into climbing after I'd given up so much for you, Alex. I couldn't play second fiddle. I had to get rid of her, or scare her off."

Alex stared at his friend pitifully. "How could you do it, Logan?" he asked. "You were my best friend."

Logan shook his head. "I don't know," he answered at last. "I just don't know.

Alex had an arm wrapped protectively around

his wife. "You need help," he said to Logan. "I only hope you get it."

When the helicopter landed at Camp Muir, Kara, Alex, Nancy, and Ned climbed out. The door to the shelter opened. Everyone greeted them warmly, including Hank and Joe, who were safe and sound. They had started down the mountain after the avalanche had passed them by.

Inside, a hot meal had been prepared. As Nancy lifted a forkful of spaghetti to her mouth, Hank cleared his throat.

"I want to apologize to you, Alex," he said gravely. "I had no right to send Lisa snooping around here."

"That's all right," Alex answered graciously. "No harm was done, and I can understand how a drop in business would make a person panic."

"Yes, well, it was still an awful thing for me to do. I want you to know that I'm sorry," Hank finished.

Alex smiled. "Apology accepted," he said. "And I'm sure there's enough climbing business around here for both of us."

"There'll be more after I write my article," Eladio said.

"I just can't believe that my best friend was trying to kill my wife," Alex said, shaking his head. "I trusted him."

"We all did," Kara said gently. "Logan and I had our differences, but I would never have guessed he was out to kill me."

"That was the point," Nancy said. "He knew that you both considered him a good friend, so he figured he could threaten Kara and not look guilty."

"But what about my car accident and Tsu's fall?"

"I can't say for sure," Nancy replied. "But I think both of those incidents were planned for Kara."

"That's right, they probably were," Kara agreed.

"Well, it's all over now," Alex said. "And I think we should celebrate with a trip to the summit tomorrow."

"All right," Ned said, pumping his fist in the air.

At twelve o'clock the next day Nancy and the rest of the group reached the summit of Mt. Rainier. The climb to the top had taken about seven hours.

"This is what makes it all worthwhile," Kara said as the group stood taking in the view. They could see for miles in every direction—the lesser mountains covered in a thick blanket of white snow, and far, far away an expanse of blue that was the Pacific Ocean. "I've climbed this mountain a hundred times, and every time I love the view a little bit more."

"Well, to tell you the truth, climbing it once might just be enough for me," Eladio said, catching his breath. "The view is fabulous, but I feel like I've just run a marathon."

"You've more than just run a marathon," Alex responded. "You've just climbed up a fourteen-thousand-foot mountain carrying nearly one-fourth of your weight on your back—in freezing temperatures."

"I'm glad you didn't put it quite that way before I decided to do a story on you," Eladio answered. "I probably would have changed my mind—or at least waited until June."

"Well, we're happy that you came," Kara said sincerely.

Standing at the crater rim bundled in her parka, Nancy felt happy and incredibly relieved at the outcome of the case.

"Thanks to you, we made it to the top," Ned

said, giving her a cold kiss on the cheek. He looked so handsome in his parka, his cheeks pink from the winter air.

"Well, it wasn't just me," Nancy replied modestly. "But I suppose I played a part in it." She sighed happily. "Isn't the view incredible?"

"It sure is," Ned replied, peering deeply into Nancy's eyes. "It's the best view I've ever seen."

Nancy's next case:

Esme Moore, America's hottest romance writer, has come to River Heights, and the rumors are swirling. She's written her autobiography, a book of true confessions, and the scandals are sure to explode off the page. But someone has vowed to kill the book—or Esme—before her revelations come to light. It's up to Nancy to find the source of the threat. Speaking of scandals, Nancy may be on the verge of starting one of her own. A handsome young River Heights detective has joined her on the case, and Nancy's beginning to wonder if romance is simply in the air. But for now, she must attend to the intrigue at hand: the web of jealousy, suspicion, and betrayal that threatens to destroy Esme Moore . . . in *Kiss and Tell*, Case #104 in The Nancy Drew Files™.

THE HARDY BOYS CASEFILES